A
JEFF RESNICK
SIX PACK

by L.L. Bartlett

 Polaris Press

OTHER BOOKS BY L. L. Bartlett

The Jeff Resnick Mysteries
(also available as audiobooks)
MURDER ON THE MIND
DEAD IN RED
CHEATED BY DEATH
BOUND BY SUGGESTION
DARK WATERS
EVOLUTION: JEFF RESNICK'S BACKSTORY

Short Stories:
WHEN THE SPIRIT MOVES YOU
BAH! HUMBUG
COLD CASE
SPOOKED!
CRYBABY
EYEWITNESS

Writing as Lorraine Bartlett

TALES OF TELENIA (Adventure-Fantasy)
(also available as audiobooks)
THRESHOLD
JOURNEY
TREACHERY (2016)

The Lotus Bay Mysteries
PANTY RAID: A TORI CANNON-KATHY GRANT MINI MYSTERY
WITH BAITED BREATH

The Victoria Square Mysteries
(also available as audiobooks)
A CRAFTY KILLING
THE WALLED FLOWER
ONE HOT MURDER
RECIPES TO DIE FOR: A VICTORIA SQUARE COOKBOOK

Short Stories:
Love & Murder: A Collection of Stories
Panty Raid: A Tori Cannon-Kathy Grant mini mystery
Blue Christmas
An Unconditional Love
Prisoner of Love
Love Heals
We're So Sorry, Uncle Albert

Writing as Lorna Barrett

The Booktown Mysteries
(also available as audiobooks)
Murder Is Binding
Bookmarked For Death
Bookplate Special
Chapter & Hearse
Sentenced To Death
Murder On The Half Shelf
Not the Killing Type
Book Clubbed
A Fatal Chapter
Title Wave

Table of Contents

FROM THE AUTHOR

It seems like I never take the easy path when it comes to anything I do. Is it that I'm just not fast on the uptake, or that I need to approach certain things in a more measured progression? I don't know. All I know is, I don't work like most authors I know. As a pantster (one who writes by the seat of her pants), I often have to go back to figure out why my characters behave the way they do. This collection of stories is a prime example.

While working on the four original books in the Jeff Resnick series (over the span of about five years—*Dead in Red* and *Dark Waters* came much later), I sometimes wrote character sketches to explore why Jeff and Richard reacted the way they did. Of course, *Cold Case* was the inspiration for *Bound By Suggestion*. I was intrigued by Dr. Krista Marsh and her interest in Jeff's psychic ability.

The next short story was *Bah Humbug* (which comes directly after *Cheated By Death*).

By this time, *Murder On The Mind* had sold, but my then-agent didn't like *Room At The Inn*. It was too "cozy" for her, and she told me to write another book. Out came *Dead In Red*. But I needed to have a bridge between it and *Cheated by Death*. That's when I wrote *When The Spirit Moves you*.

It was several years later that I decided my agent had been wrong. I knew that people would enjoy *Room at the Inn*, which has a cozy setting (a Vermont inn), but there was nothing cozy about the murder and Jeff's investigation.

I've been a writing maniac for the past several years, but after *Dark Waters*, I couldn't fit a full-length Jeff novel in the writing schedule, which was why I decided to write a few shorter pieces. I wrote *Spooked!* longhand during the long car ride from Rochester, New York to St. Pete Beach, Florida. The timing was great. I finished it on Halloween.

2

Sometimes I give myself a Christmas present. I let myself write a story that I know I would enjoy reading. I wrote *Crybaby* in December 2014. Why did I need a spiritual lift? My mother had been diagnosed with terminal cancer. Writing that story kept me going.

Dealing with a loved-one's illness can be extremely depressing. I needed to cope with her impending death, and Jeff still had issues to deal with. I knew he couldn't move forward with his life until he dealt with the death of his wife, Shelley. It was a difficult story to write because I wasn't writing with joy anymore. I had a book to deliver to my traditional publisher, and I would force myself to work on it (and, oddly enough, I don't think you can tell that I wrote it during a long depression). I only allowed myself to work on *Eyewitness* after I accomplished the daily word quota on that novel. Some days I wrote 25 to 100 words; some days I only wrote a sentence, but I finally finished *Eyewitness* in late May, just three weeks before my mother's death. She never had a chance to read it.

Will there be more Jeff novels and short stories?

Just try to stop me from writing them.

TIMELINE

The Jeff Resnick Mysteries
(Stories in order)

MURDER ON THE MIND
DEAD IN RED
    When The Spirit Moves You
ROOM AT THE INN
CHEATED BY DEATH
    Bah! Humbug
    Cold Case (the inspiration for Bound By Suggestion)
BOUND BY SUGGESTION
DARK WATERS
    Spooked!
    Crybaby
    Eyewitness
EVOLUTION: Jeff Resnick's Backstory

Jeff Resnick's curiosity is piqued when he sees a sign advertising psychic readings. At first he's sure the medium is a fake, but then his funny feelings lead him to suspect that a murder has taken place in the dilapidated house where Madam Zahara holds her readings. Just who died and how? And why is Jeff compelled to look for bodies buried in the medium's yard?

WHEN THE SPIRIT MOVES YOU

I'd passed the hulking, ramshackle house every few days for the last three months on my way home from my girlfriend Maggie Brennan's house. The yard hadn't seen the services of a lawnmower or weed wacker in quite some time. But it was the glowing pink-and-green neon sign that seemed to call to me: PSYCHIC $10.

Since I got whacked on the head with a Reggie Jackson baseball bat last winter, I can sometimes sense people's emotions. And sometimes I know stuff about them, and it's usually not good. I don't consider myself a psychic. No way. In fact, I've come to view that as a dirty word. But being mugged by a couple of teenage thugs changed me. Slammed my brains into my thick skull—mooshed them up a bit—and . . . now I'm not the same as I was before. Not the same at all.

It was all still pretty new to me, and I wasn't sure I always trusted the feelings—insights—that came to me. I mean, I did—and I didn't want to.

But that day I had an extra ten-dollar bill in my wallet and I decided—why not test it? If the person advertising such a trait was for real, I might find a kindred spirit. If not—okay, when you're broke, ten bucks is a lot of money, but I had a roof over my head, a part-time job and, thanks to the generosity of my older half brother, I was nowhere near starving. Maybe it was the neon that seduced me on that hot August afternoon when I found myself pulling into the gravel drive.

The sign on the lawn said "For Entertainment Only," but I was pretty sure the gullible would expect something more than that. And why was I so intrigued anyway? My friend Sophie Levin was like me. The old Polish lady didn't like the word psychic either. She read auras—or as she put it, she "saw colors" and then knew things.

I looked through the car's passenger-side window at what once might have been a lovely home. Hard times had fallen on the old two-story house. Was it supposed to be a poor man's Tara? The Corinthian columns that held up the porch roof were rotted at the base. Flaked paint chips the size of oatmeal cookies hung from the weathered clapboards. A rusty Buick LeSabre with current plates sat parked at the side of the house. Apparently psychic-for-hire was not a particularly lucrative proposition.

I got out of my car, my footsteps crunching on the gravel as I made my way to the porch steps. They creaked under my feet. Were they rotted enough to collapse or should I trust them to hold my weight?

They held.

The porch floorboards groaned under me as I shifted my weight and raised my hand to knock on the old screen door. A woman's voice called out, "I've been waiting for you. What took you so long?"

The words were disconcerting. I'd only decided to drop in on a whim. Or maybe that was part of her shtick.

I opened the wooden screen door and stepped inside. The interior didn't look much better than the exterior, but at least it was neat and tidy. A broad staircase wound up to the second floor. Only a few of its balusters were missing. The entry's floor was in desperate need of sanding and refinishing, and some of the old oak was warped and a large portion of it was discolored from water. A glance at the stained ceiling told me where the problem had originated. Probably from a bathroom.

"In here," the female voice called again.

I crossed the entryway to a side parlor and shuddered. Something in that room was not right. From her position behind a small square table, the woman could see straight through the window should any customers pull up the drive and approach the steps.

The room had little charm. The cracked and chipped brick hearth was in as sad a shape as the mantle, which had once been painted white. Instead of a fire, seven or eight white vanilla-scented pillar candles of different heights glowed in the old fireplace, and appeared to be the only source of heat or light in the gloomy room.

Two sheet-covered side chairs flanked the mantle, but instead of shabby chic, they just looked shabby—as did the faded wallpaper which, like the ceiling in the entry-way, had its share of water stains around the windows. A tall, newish cabinet held up the wall behind me. No doubt a TV was stashed behind the closed doors. I'd bet the days were long and the customers few and far between, and soap operas and game shows helped to pass the hours.

"Please, sit," she invited, and waved a hand at the worn upholstered chair before her.

I did as asked and, apart from feeling foolish, a growing disquiet seemed to radiate through me. I tried to shake it off and concentrated on the woman before me.

Talk about adopting a stereotype. The table was covered in a couple of layers of jewel-toned tablecloths and what looked like a lacy white shawl draped on top. A massive crystal ball sat in the middle of the table, and in front of the woman was a neatly stacked deck of worn Tarot cards.

I looked up into the woman's piercing blue eyes. She must have been in her early fifties, overweight, with a lined face and jet-black, shoulder-length wavy hair held back from her left ear by a rhinestone dragonfly clip.

Seated behind the table like that, I could only see that she had on a white blouse with a black shawl drawn over her shoulders. But I suspected her outfit included a long dark skirt hidden beneath the table. Despite the candles, the pong of cigarette smoke still hung in the air. A trace of white on the edge of the table told me she'd hastily ditched her ashtray—probably onto her lap.

"I ask that my clients pay in advance, if you wouldn't mind."

"Sure." I grabbed the wallet from my left back pocket, withdrew the ten-dollar bill and offered it to her. She grabbed the money and stowed it under the table.

"Now, how can I help you, Mister—?"

Help me?

"Resnick. Jeffrey Resnick," I supplied.

Her eyes flashed and seemed to give me a quick once-over—evaluating me, and perhaps my stupidity factor.

"I saw your sign and wondered what you could tell me about . . . things."

That sounded lame, but I really didn't know what I expected. Probably just to find out what kind of cock-n-bull story she'd hand me. I get vibes from people, and so far the only vibe I got from this lady was that she had just robbed me of ten bucks.

"I can contact the spirit world in a number of ways. Via the crystal, the Tarot, or through my animal guide. How would you like me to proceed, Mr. Resnick?"

Animal guide? Cat? Horse? Rhinoceros? "I have no preference."

She nodded, moved the cards to one side, and pulled the crystal ball toward her. Leaning forward, she held her hands inches over the glass orb and gazed into it, her blue eyes going wide, her whole act looking kind of hokey to me. The ball's short gold-tone base was peeling on the side closest to me, not unlike the paint and wallpaper around us.

"I see you've fallen on hard times," she said, still gazing into the ball. She was one to talk. And did she have the gift of clairvoyance or had she deduced that by the wreck I'd parked outside her window and the fact my shoes needed a shine?

"Go on," I urged her.

"You have not been well."

Another brilliant deduction. After the mugging that had almost killed me five months before, I'd lost weight and had never gained it back. I wasn't exactly gaunt, but I could have used another five or ten pounds to help me stand upright on a blustery day.

"What else do you see?" I asked.

She seemed to be puzzling over the crystal for an awfully long time and I was getting antsy. This wasn't much of a show for ten bucks.

It was then I noticed movement over her shoulder and in the darkest corner of the room. I squinted. I hadn't imagined it. A forty-something white man stood there. He had brown hair, and a really bad haircut, and was dressed in dark slacks and a plaid flannel shirt. Funny thing was, I hadn't seen or heard him enter the room.

The feeling of disquiet grew within me.

I was about to ask the woman who the guy was, but he held up his right hand and pressed his index finger to his lips as though to shush me.

I sat back in my chair and frowned. I hadn't expected an expanded audience at this little performance.

"I'm curious about this house. Have you lived here long?" I asked the woman.

She waved a hand in the air as though batting away a pesky insect. "That has no bearing on your future—or your past," she said with the slightest bit of an edge to her tone. "I see trouble ahead for you."

"What kind of trouble?"

"With the police."

Oh yeah? "A traffic ticket?"

She shook her head. "Something much more serious."

As I'd already helped track down two killers in the short time I'd been back in Buffalo, I found her observation oddly disturbing. I'd figured she was a blatant fraud. Now I wasn't so sure.

I looked back to the corner of the room but the guy in the plaid shirt was gone.

How? He hadn't made a sound and I swear he never walked past the fortuneteller's table to escape the room.

Where the hell had he gone?

Thanks to my stop for psychic entertainment, I was late getting home for dinner that night. I live in the apartment over the garage on my brother's property, and I often join him and his wife for meals at their house, although "house" was a bit of a misnomer. Mansion wasn't quite right, either, but came pretty close. At any rate, it was a comfortable arrangement.

That night my sister-in-law, Brenda, had roasted a chicken, and had included all the fixings. Whipped potatoes, homemade sage-and-onion stuffing, peas, salad, and a bowl of jellied cranberry sauce, along with a plate mounded with grocery store dinner rolls.

"Are we doing a trial run for Thanksgiving?" I asked, taking in the table laden with food—a heavy meal for such a warm weekday evening.

"I thought it would be nice to have a hearty dinner for once. Help yourself to a beer and sit down," she said.

I grabbed a bottle of Labatt Blue from the fridge and took my usual seat at the table.

"So, what's new with you?" my older, half-brother Richard Alpert asked as he helped himself to a dinner roll.

I passed the butter. "I stopped off on the way home to visit the psychic on Route 5."

"What did you do that for?" he asked, annoyed, and hacked off a gob of butter, spreading it across his roll.

"Entertainment value only—although she didn't put on much of an act for ten bucks."

"What did she tell you? I assume it was a woman psychic," Brenda said, sounding much more interested.

I nodded and helped myself to one of the chicken thighs, a scoop of potatoes, and some peas. "She was a walking—or rather sitting—stereotype of the trade. And she didn't say much. Just that I'd fallen on hard times and had been ill."

"It doesn't take a psychic to deduce that," Richard said reasonably.

Amen. I decided not to mention her threat about trouble with the cops. Richard worries like an old lady about such things.

"Are you going to go again? Can I come along?" Brenda asked eagerly.

"You're *not* going," Richard said.

"You can't tell me where I can and can't go," Brenda countered defiantly.

"You're right. But I strongly suggest you *don't go*. It would be a waste of time and money. Pass the potatoes, please."

I handed him the bowl. "I am going back, and no you can't come, Brenda. There was something sinister about that place."

"Then why would you want to go back?" Richard asked and chased a couple of peas around his dinner plate.

"I've got a feeling something bad happened there."

He looked at me with disapproval. "All the more reason for you to stay away."

"What kind of bad?" Brenda asked eagerly. She reads mysteries—loves them, in fact.

"Violence. Maybe . . . a murder. I'm not sure."

Her expression soured and she turned her gaze back to her husband. "You're right, Richard—I don't think I want to go anymore. And you shouldn't either," Brenda cautioned me. "We all know that nothing good ever comes from your vibes."

That wasn't true. Matt Sumner's killer would have escaped justice if I hadn't looked into his death. Same with the person who murdered Walt Kaplan. Of course, it was Richard, not me, who'd paid dearly during both those encounters. I would go this little adventure on my own.

"You've hardly touched your dinner," Brenda chided me. "It's getting cold."

Thinking about that house, that woman, and the disappearing man made me lose what little appetite I'd had.

That night—and the next—my dreams were haunted by the chubby medium and the silent man from the eerie house on Route 5. Indistinct images of those two people and that creepy house played and replayed through my sleeping hours. Her speaking nonsense, and him saying nothing but listening to everything.

When disturbing stuff bothered me, I knew the only place I could go to and talk about it with someone who really understood was in a little bakery on Main Street. It was kind of like Brigadoon. Sometimes it was there—and sometimes it wasn't. Well, the bakery was always there—but the person I sought wasn't always available.

It was nearly three o'clock in the morning and Main Street was empty as I jaywalked toward the bakery. Sure enough, the light was on in the back of the shop. I didn't even have to ring the bell. A silhouette tottered toward the door and my octogenarian friend Sophie opened the door to let me in. "You're late," she said in greeting, and offered her cheek for a kiss.

"Sorry. I wasn't sure I was coming."

"You always say that," she grumbled and pivoted to return to the back room. She moved stiffly, as though in pain.

"Are you okay?" I asked, concerned.

"It's this stinking humidity . . . it always cranks up my arthritis," she complained.

As usual, the bakery smelled incredibly good. The mingled aromas of bread, cookies, and cakes filled the air. Also as usual, Sophie had set the small Formica table with chipped plates. She'd placed large sugar cookies on a bigger plate in the center of the table.

I took my customary seat as Sophie checked the progress of the kettle on the hotplate that sat on a shelf over the sink. I'd warned her time and time again that it was a dangerous arrangement, but she always blew me off. For such a smart woman, she had a blind spot when it came to her personal safety.

"So what brings you here tonight?" she asked.

"Have you ever seen a ghost?"

Sophie picked up the kettle and paused before turning to face me. She'd make me tea, hot chocolate, or instant coffee—depending on the weather. Tonight it was instant coffee. The stuff tasted like shit—not that I'd tell her that.

"I think I have . . . but . . . I really can't be sure," she admitted, and poured the hot water into mugs. She set the mugs down on the table, took her seat, and then pushed the powdered creamer toward me. "What makes you think you've seen a ghost."

"I didn't say I had."

She leveled a stony glare at me. "You didn't say you hadn't, either."

I told her about my visit to the Route 5 medium. With every sentence her expression grew more sour.

"That was a waste of your time *and* money," she muttered. "These people are all fakes."

"You're not a fake."

"And neither are you. But we don't go around advertising our gifts and trying to make money from desperate people, either."

"Well, it seemed like I needed to go there. And now I feel like I need to go back."

She shook her head. "Nothing but trouble can come from this."

"Trouble for whom?" I asked.

"You—in the short run."

"And someone else in the long run?"

She shrugged. "So, tell me about this so-called ghost."

"There's not much to tell. I don't even know if he *is* a ghost. It's just . . . the place gives off weird vibes and this guy suddenly showed up and then just as quickly disappeared."

"Could you see right through him?" she asked.

It was my turn to shake my head.

"He looked solid?" she persisted.

I nodded.

"In movies, ghosts always look transparent."

"That's movies. We're talking real life."

"Not if he's dead," Sophie pointed out. She reached for a cookie, placed it on her plate, and then broke it in half, nibbling on one of the pieces. "Are you afraid of meeting a ghost?"

I'd seen some pretty weird stuff since I'd been bonked on the head with a baseball bat and became . . . different. "I don't think I'm afraid as much as . . . worried."

"Why?"

"What if this guy is depending on me to discover what happened to him?"

"Is that what you hope to accomplish by going back to see this fraud of a fortuneteller? Figuring out why he died?"

"That's just it. I'm not sure. But if this guy died because someone helped him to the afterlife or . . . whatever

. . . shouldn't somebody try to help him move on?"

"Has he asked you for help?"

I shook my head. "He hasn't said a word."

"Then how do you know he even needs help?"

I grabbed a cookie from the plate, broke it into about six pieces and shoved one of them into my mouth, chewing fast. It tasted pretty good, but I didn't care. I was wondering why I cared about some dead guy I'd never known in life.

But for some reason I *did* care. Shouldn't that be enough?

I voiced the question.

Sophie shrugged. "I guess if somebody did me in, I'd hope that somebody cared enough to find out why. But why does it always have to be *you*?"

"Maybe nobody else knows the guy is dead."

Sophie sipped her coffee, and then picked up the other half of her cookie. "Then I guess you'd better do something to find that out."

And so it was two days after my first visit that I returned to the decrepit old house, which looked no better on my second visit than it had on my first. The weather had deteriorated and a gentle rain had been falling for most of the day. When I knocked at the old screen door I could see a number of plastic pails and bowls had been placed in strategic places around the entryway to catch drips. Still, it suddenly occurred to me that maybe the dark stains on the floor might not be due to a leaky bathroom after all.

"I knew you'd be back," called the woman fortuneteller from within. I then realized that I hadn't thought to ask her name the last time I'd been there, and she hadn't introduced herself, either. "Come in," she encouraged.

Sure she was friendly. She knew if I walked through

the door she would be able to order a small cheese-and-pepperoni pizza for dinner. If she'd already had one other customer that day, she could upgrade to a medium with enough left over for lunch the next day and give the delivery guy a tip, too.

"Sit down, Mr. Resnick," she said, waving a hand to encourage me to take the seat opposite her. Today she wore a sleeveless blue shell top, but the black shawl was still draped over her shoulders—no doubt for effect. The oppressive humidity in that room wasn't improved by the presence of a large white oscillating fan that moved listlessly from left to right.

I sat down and, without a word, she held out her hand to receive her fee upfront. I counted out ten one dollar bills. I'd had good tips that day while tending bar at the Whole Nine Yards—a job I'd held for a little over two months.

"And why have you returned so soon?" the woman asked.

"What you told me the other day intrigued me," I lied. "I wanted to know more."

It had been the right thing to say. The corners of her mouth quirked into a smile. She reached for her crystal ball and pulled it closer.

Again movement in the shadows drew my attention. Once again the guy with the bad haircut stood in the corner, wearing the same plaid shirt—a garment much too heavy for such a hot, humid day—and I swear he hadn't been there when I'd entered the room. He smiled, waggled his eyebrows a la Groucho Marx, and gave me a four-fingered wave with his right hand. He looked pretty substantial to me.

I turned my attention back to the woman. "I'm sorry, but I don't know your name."

"You may call me Madam Zahara."

Madam Zahara? O-kay.

"Madam Zahara, do you live here alone?"

She hesitated before answering. "Most of the time. My son comes and goes. He's a long-distance truck driver. He'll probably return tonight."

Had she added the last to warn me off should I be some kind of robber or rapist?

If she was in her fifties, her son was probably in his twenties or thirties. The guy in the corner had to be at least forty. He turned to look out the nearest window to the weed-strewn yard beyond. I got the feeling that before I headed for home I should probably take a walk around that yard. For some reason I wasn't quite sure I understood, I was *supposed* to look around that yard before I headed home. And I had a feeling I might find something I would definitely not like finding.

Once again Madam Zahara held her hands over her crystal ball as she gazed within its depths. "Ahh, today I see—"

"Death?" I supplied.

Her brow wrinkled and she frowned. "No. Why would you say that?" she asked, sounding frightened.

"Because there's a darkness that hovers over this house. Surely you've felt it."

Her blue eyes widened in suspicion. "Why do you say that?"

My gaze traveled up to the ceiling and ran back to the stained floor in the entryway. I had originally assumed the wood had been marred by dripping water over a long period of time. But now I thought I knew better. That knowledge made the humidity suddenly seem ten times as oppressive.

"You told me on Tuesday that an encounter with the police would be in my future. I think you were right."

"Is there something *you're* guilty of that *you've* been hiding?" she asked with a bit of a smirk.

"Not me. I think it's you."

She sat back, taking umbrage. "I don't know what you mean."

"Don't you?" I asked, unsure why I'd taken the offensive.

"No," she said quite firmly.

I heaved a heavy sigh and looked back at the guy who stood silent in the darkened corner of the room. He nodded and then raised a hand to make a slashing motion across his throat.

"How long have you lived here?" I asked.

"Ten years. And why the hell would you care?" She was definitely on the defensive. "Look, I think you'd better leave." She pushed the stack of ones back toward me, but I shook my head.

"I have a feeling you're going to need them. In fact, I think you're going to need a lot more than ten dollars to hire someone to tackle your defense."

"What are you talking about?" she demanded.

"The shallow grave out in the side yard. There's a body buried there—or what's left of a body. The big stain in the entryway isn't from water damage. It's blood."

She rose to stand, much shorter than she'd appeared sitting behind the table. "I think you'd better leave. Now."

"I agree. But if you don't call the cops about this, I will."

For a moment—just a moment—I was suddenly afraid. I'd made a baseless accusation. I had nothing more than a gut feeling to go with and she had called my bluff. Momentarily. But then a gush of remorse and sorrow threatened to engulf me. It wasn't my own . . . it belonged to her.

"Call the police," I said. "This has been a heavy burden on your soul for a long time."

Her lower lip trembled for a few seconds before she burst into tears.

"I think I should go now," I said and rose from my seat. "But I'm not going very far—and if I don't see a police cruiser park in your drive within the next half hour, I'm going to call them and that would complicate my life. You don't *want* to complicate my life," I told her in a tone I'd never used when talking with a woman.

Suddenly her fear shifted from whatever she'd done to whatever she thought I might be capable of doing. It wasn't a pleasant state of mind for me to accept.

She took a ragged breath and pulled a clunky old cell phone from her skirt pocket and hit three buttons—911. She lifted the phone to her ear and cleared her throat. "I'd like to report a murder."

I looked across to the corner of the room. The man who stood there smiled, lifted his right hand to give me a thumbs up, and then slowly dissolved into thin air.

True to my word, I'd pulled out of her driveway and drove a quarter of a mile down the road to turn around. Then I'd doubled back and parked in the used car lot directly across the road from the creepy old house to wait for the police cruiser to arrive.

I waited and waited. After more than an hour it was apparent that no cop car would arrive. She'd stiffed me. She'd pressed the correct buttons on her phone, said the words I'd expected her to say, and scammed me good. And obviously my best Clint Eastwood threat had not been believed for—sure enough—it was a pizza delivery-man who arrived, not a cop.

I started my car, pulled out of the dealership, and headed for home.

Once there, I hit the button on the remote, the garage door opened, and I parked my car. Before I could close the door and head upstairs to my own place, I saw Brenda hanging out the back door of the big house, waving me to come over and join them for dinner. Since I'd guzzled the last of my twelve-pack and had nothing but a blue box of mac and cheese in the cupboard, I figured why not?

"You're late again," Brenda accused as I entered their kitchen. This time she was cooking pasta. A bag of frozen shrimp sat on the counter, accompanied by a small dish of freshly chopped garlic. Scampi was on the menu that night.

"You went back to that psychic, didn't you?" Richard accused from his seat at the kitchen table.

I sat down opposite him. "Guilty as charged."

He shook his head and took a sip of the scotch and soda that had been sitting before him.

"Want a beer?" Brenda offered me.

I shook my head. "I think something stronger might be called for."

She sighed, but stepped over to the cabinet that held the kitchen liquor, hauling out a bottle of Maker's Mark. She poured me a couple of fingers worth, tossed in some ice and soda, and handed it to me. Ahh—that hit the spot.

"And?" Richard prompted.

"The so-called psychic is hiding something. I'm pretty sure there's a body buried in the yard."

"Oh, God," Richard groused and downed what was left in his glass with one gulp.

"I was going to search the yard before I left, but the bitch called my bluff. I'd told her to call the cops and she produced a cell phone and pretended to do it. Only they never showed."

"So what happens next?" Richard asked.

"Like I said, I think there's a body buried in the yard. No one's going to believe me unless I can come up with some kind of proof.

"I don't like the sound of this," Richard said, and why

would he? Thanks to my escapades he'd been shot, and now had the death threat of HIV hanging over his head.

"Don't worry," I said. "I'm not asking you to come with me—in fact, I don't want you to come. But if I can bring back some kind of evidence that you can identify as being human—say a bone—maybe you could go with me to the Clarence Police Department when I report it."

"Do you honestly think I'm going to let you go digging for evidence alone?" Richard asked.

"Why are either of you even *considering* going to that house?" Brenda cried.

I gave her what I hoped was a patient look. "Brenda, if a murder has taken place, then justice needs to be served." Geeze, I sounded like some kind of sanctimonious asshole right off a TV drama.

"And why is it always *you* that needs to be the catalyst for justice? Why can't somebody else play Superman?" Now she sounded like Sophie.

"No red cape and blue tights?" I suggested.

She glared at me.

"What made you suspicious of this woman in the first place?"

"I got weird vibes going into that house. When I asked her about it, she blew me off."

Richard frowned and shook the ice in his glass, as though hoping Brenda would take the hint and make him another drink. She didn't. Finally he got up and poured his own Scotch. "Okay, say the woman killed that guy. What are the odds she'll be armed if you show up?" he asked as he slopped Lagavulin over ice.

"I wouldn't put it past her. The entry was stained with what looked like a lot of blood."

"You two are not seriously thinking of going out there tonight to investigate, are you?" Brenda asked.

"She knows I know something," I pointed out. "She knows she's got to hide the evidence."

"And what if she's digging up the evidence when you arrive?" Brenda insisted.

"That would be the perfect time to call the cops and have *them* catch her in the act."

"And if she doesn't dig up the evidence?" she demanded.

"Then we can call the cops." I paused. Hadn't I already decided Richard shouldn't participate, and yet here I was including him in my plans. "It's a win-win situation."

Brenda shook her head. "Oh, no-no-no. Things never work out that neatly."

"Maybe, maybe not. But we've got to give it a try," Richard agreed.

"No, you don't. Call the police!"

"But I've got no tangible proof. They don't treat gut feelings as real evidence."

The pasta threatened to boil over and Brenda turned to tend to it.

I sipped my bourbon and looked at my physician brother. He already had a potential death threat hanging over his head, thanks to being exposed to a bloodied, high-risk patient with no latex protection between his hands and the dying man. Still, there was no denying the longing in his eyes, begging to be involved—to feel alive—especially at a time when he might be looking at his own mortality.

I wanted to protect my brother, but could I deny him the chance to live at a time when he wasn't sure what his future might bring?

"What's the plan?" Richard asked.

Brenda glared at him, but I sensed that she understood that it was up to Richard to decide his own fate.

"For now, we assess the situation. There's no reason we have to hurry on this." And yet as soon as I said it I knew that time was running out for finding the remains

... and that guy in the plaid shirt. I was sure it was him buried in a shallow grave alongside the house. Had I really seen a ghost? Had whatever was left of the man been hanging around the place in hopes that someone would uncover his fate—find him—and finally see that he was properly laid to rest? Had Madam Zahara killed him or had her seldom-home son done the deed? And what was the dead man's relationship with the two of them? Lover? Husband? Father? Hapless mark?

Richard raised his glass, gazing at the amber liquid within it. "There's no time like the present. Let's have dinner and then go find your evidence," he said to me. He lowered his glass, took a sip, and then shifted his gaze toward Brenda. "You could come with us."

She shook her head. "Not on your life. I'll be here, keeping the home fires burning. And if you aren't home at a reasonable hour, I'll call the cops and report you as missing persons."

"You're overreacting," I told her.

"Oh yeah? We'll see," she said, glowering at me.

Since Brenda was a kindred spirit, and I meant that literally—she had a limited sixth sense about such things—I took her warning seriously and wished to God I hadn't mentioned anything about this mess to them. Richard felt some kind of misplaced guilt about my teenaged years spent in his home, and the lack of understanding and concern his grandparents felt on my behalf. In retrospect, I didn't blame them. I reminded them of our mother, a woman they'd disapproved of—despised, actually. That they'd allowed me to live in their home after our mother's death, and for the better part of four years, had to gall them. They had loved Richard enough to put up with me.

No one had loved *me*.

I shook my head to dislodge all the crap from so long ago, but somehow it always seemed to come back to haunt me at the worst moments.

Brenda got up and put a big skillet on the stove before she took a stick of butter out of the fridge to sauté the shrimp. She'd make sure her troops were well fed before they marched off to . . . battle? No, we weren't looking for a fight. But what we found might be a casualty of a domestic war. I was pretty sure if we dug in just the right spot, we'd find bones—and maybe the remnants of a plaid flannel shirt.

I drained my Maker's Mark and got up to make another. I had a feeling I'd better fortify myself. What lay ahead could be pretty gruesome. Or was I being overly melodramatic? After all, I had no evidence—nothing but a gut feeling to go by. Still, gut feelings had served me well in the recent past.

I poured that fine bourbon and took a sip. This would be my last drink before we hit the road, but I had a feeling that bottle might run dry upon our return.

The clouds had dissipated, but thanks to Buffalo's light-polluted sky, no stars broke through the artificial haze. Richard had had a glass or two of wine with his scampi, so I elected to drive us to the psychic's neighborhood.

I parked my car on a side street four blocks from the house and took out a shovel from the trunk of my car. I carried it while Richard hefted the large orange flashlight that usually lived under his kitchen sink.

"So how did the guy die?" Richard asked as we headed west on the cracked and weed-studded sidewalk.

"Blunt trauma to the skull," I said and realized that the phrase perfectly described my own injury five months before. Was that the common denominator that connected me with the flannel-clad victim?

The streetlamps cast bluish shadows. We walked the rest of the way—side-by-side—in silence. If anyone saw me with that shovel, what would they think? Would they call 911 or just assume I was a nutcase on the loose? Luckily traffic was light and none of the cars that passed seemed to notice us as we trekked down the concrete path.

Finally I grabbed Richard's arm, pulling him to a stop, and we took in the psychic's residence. Except for a flickering blue light in one of the upstairs rooms—a rerun of Survivor?—the big old house was dark. I couldn't even see the sign that advertised the medium's services.

"Creepy," Richard whispered.

"You ought to see the inside."

We walked past the gravel drive and once out of the glow of lamplight darted into the home's weed-strewn side yard.

"Goddamnit, you didn't tell me the place hadn't been mown all summer," Richard groused as our arrival seemed to have rousted a swarm of hungry mosquitoes.

"What's a little malaria between friends," I said, swatting at my bare arms and wishing I'd worn a jacket. "And what are you bitching for anyway? All you have to do is hold the flashlight. I'm the idiot who's got to do the digging."

"So start digging."

Sound advice, but I had no idea where to start. "Give me a minute, willya?"

"A minute," he said testily.

I shut my eyes and cleared my mind, hoping I'd get some kind of vibe from the dead guy. I heard Richard slapping at mosquitoes and swearing under his breath.

Maybe I needed to roam around the yard. Maybe if I trooped across the area in a kind of grid pattern I would get weird vibes, literally stumble across the gravesite, dig down a foot or so, find the victim and—voila—justice would be served.

Of course the flaw in that plan was proving Madam

Zahara or her son had killed the guy and buried him there. And what was their motive supposed to be, anyway?

"Have you got a plan or are we just going to stand here and be bitten until we come down with West Nile virus?" Richard asked.

"I'd better walk the property. Maybe then I'll know where to start digging." I could see Richard's form in silhouette. He shook his head as though perturbed. "Why don't you go stand on the sidewalk until I call for you. That way you won't get bitten as much."

"I'll do that," he said. "The last thing I need right now is another blood-born virus." He stalked off.

I looked around the shadowy yard wondering which way I ought to go. It didn't matter. I chose to start at the farthest, darkest corner and wished I'd asked Richard to hold the shovel while I used the flashlight.

No sooner had I gone five feet when the toe of my sneakered foot got caught in a hole. The shovel went flying and I fell flat on my face, wrenching my knee. "Goddammit," I swore as I grabbed at my leg, rolling onto my side. My movements had jostled a whole new swarm of mosquitoes, who seemed to zero in on my face and neck. I could feel them crawling all over me and slapped and cursed at them in anger.

"Will you shut up!" Richard whispered loudly.

"I just fell in a friggin' hole," I hissed back.

"Well, be more careful."

That was easy for him to say, he had the flashlight.

I groped for the shovel and used it to haul myself upright before gingerly putting weight on my throbbing knee. It let me know it was not happy, but it didn't give out on me, either. I took a fortifying breath to steady myself and opened my mind as I hobbled up and down the yard.

The night air was cool and damp—clammy—and I

shivered. In fact, I stopped and felt downright frozen. The saying "cold as the grave" came back to me.

"I think I found it," I called to Richard.

No answer.

"Hey, you still there?"

"Oh, shit," I heard him say out loud.

"What's the matter?"

Before he could answer, a police car—with lights flashing—skidded to a halt in front of the yard.

"Oh, shit," I said as the officer jumped out of the cruiser, trained a light on the yard until he found me, and then drew his gun.

"Hands up!" he shouted.

I did as I was told, still with shovel in hand. "Something wrong, officer?" I asked, trying to sound cheerful.

"Yeah, you're trespassing. Put down the shovel and drop to the ground."

I tossed the shovel aside and fell to the grass, unleashing another horde of mosquitoes and wondered if the town lock-up provided Calamine lotion for its prisoners.

Brenda whacked a jumbo egg on the side of the hot skillet, then dropped its contents into the spattering butter. "Of all the stupid, lame-brained ideas . . . ."

"Hey, as a person with a brain injury, I resent that remark," I said, and took a sip of my coffee. It was nine-thirty, and I'd had to sit in jail until first thing that morning, waiting for a judge to set bail and for Richard to come and collect me. He'd been smart and ducked behind an arborvitae when the cop arrested me the night before. I didn't hold a grudge. Why should he get in trouble for one of my funny feelings? And I promised to pay him back . . . one day . . . for making my bail.

The toast popped up and Brenda grabbed it, first

slathering butter and then raspberry jam on it before depositing it on my plate.

"Hey, what about me?" Richard complained.

I picked up one of the slices and dropped it on his plate. He nodded his thanks, scooped it up and took a bite—quite satisfied.

"And what's next on your agenda?" Brenda asked, sounding thoroughly annoyed.

I took another sip of my coffee before answering. "What I should have done first. Research the house. See who owns it. My guess is the dead guy. I've got a feeling Madam Zahara and her son have been squatting for some time."

"How can you prove that?" Richard asked, and took another bite of his toast.

"First I'd need to find out if the real owner has been seen in the past few years, which is what I should have done before we went blundering over there last night. I'll start with the county tax records to see who owns that house and who's been paying the taxes for the last few years. Next I'll see what else I can find out about the owner."

"Who says it was the owner that died? Couldn't it have been one of Madam Zahara's customers?"

I nodded. "If that's the case, I might be looking at a dead end from the start. My gut's telling me there's a paper trail to follow—but first I have to go looking for it."

"Be my guest," Richard said, polishing off the last of his toast.

"When I've pulled it all together, perhaps you'd like to be a witness when I present my evidence."

"And just who are you going to present it to?" he asked.

I picked up my cup. That was a good question. Clearly confronting Madam Zahara hadn't done the trick. But was a cop going to believe me?

Probably not.

But then I did have a friend at *The Buffalo News*. He might want to play with a missing-person story. And if he set the ball rolling, the Clarence PD might just pick it up.

I'd just have to wait and see.

But first, breakfast.

Since I wasn't scheduled to work, I spent the rest of that day on my computer in air-conditioned comfort while Brenda and Richard took off for the country club to sweat their way through a few rounds of golf.

First, thanks to the fact that the Erie County tax records were posted online, I found out the property on Route 5, which was also known as Main Street, was owned by one Fred Butterfield. Next up, I looked for every Fred Butterfield I could find, in case the owner was an absentee landlord. There were four of them in the greater Buffalo area. I had no idea how long the guy in the plaid shirt had been dead, so I wasn't sure which one I was looking for—at least at first. I discounted the one who was ninety-six and another who was six years old. That left two.

I Googled the name and came up with over five million, one hundred and eighty thousand results (in less than 2 seconds—not bad). I narrowed that down by adding Buffalo, NY to the search parameters, and winnowed it down to a mere seventy-two. It took another twenty minutes to go through that list. I found hits on only one of the guys on the tax records, who'd been a football sensation back in high school. Next stop: Facebook.

I had to go through a whole page of men by that name before I narrowed it down to two, but both of them were listed on that social network as living in the Buffalo area. Now to figure out which one was the dead guy. Not such an easy task, since one of the profile pictures was of Popeye the Sailor and the other was a 1989 orange Corvette.

Since I wasn't their "friend," their personal info pages weren't available to me. I couldn't friend them as myself—Madam Zahara knew my name and wasn't likely to approve my friendship request—so I went to Google and set up a phony email address, then went back to Facebook and set up a new account. And why hadn't it occurred to me to do this before now? I had a feeling I'd be able to use this bogus name and history for snooping in the future.

While I waited to see if my friend requests would be granted, I studied their info pages, but neither had allowed much information to be made available to non-friends.

Gut feeling told me the picture of the Corvette represented Mr. Plaid Shirt, although from the looks of his clothing and his hair, and the condition of the home on Main Street, he'd fallen on hard times long before his demise. That made the idea of someone killing him for that crappy house even more appalling.

To kill time, I friended a bunch of Buffalo institutions, including the library, the Bills, the Sabres, and any other sports-affiliated things I could think of, a few restaurants, and microbreweries, figuring what the hell—it would give my fake persona a little credibility.

I Googled Madam Zahara and found her listed in the Buffalo online phone directory—she'd even paid for an ad—but that didn't tell me who she really was or what her connection to Fred Butterfield was.

It was after three and I already had twenty friends when I looked back to my profile page to see that Mr. Corvette Butterfield was now my friend, too. I clicked onto his pictures. Bingo! There he was in a number of shots, first looking some twenty years younger with said orange Corvette, and then a few of him looking pretty much as he had when I'd seen him at Madam Zahara's. He'd apparently never had the opportunity to become older.

I clicked back to his wall and found that his last post was made just two days before. "Watching the Mets on TV." I did a quick Google search and found the team had played two days before. (They'd lost—five to three.)

So, who was updating the dead guy's page—Madam Zahara or her long-distant trucking son? And when it came down to it—I had no proof that either of them had done anything wrong, and no real proof that Fred Butterfield was actually dead. Just that funny feeling in my gut that I had learned to trust during the past five months.

I figured I'd gone about as far as I could go on my own without doing some face-to-face interviews and possibly stirring up a hornet's nest, so I called my friend Sam Nielson at *The Buffalo News*.

Sam and I go back to high school days. He was the editor of the school newspaper and I took the photos. We didn't talk much back then, but we're now . . . maybe not friends, but we had a mutual understanding when it came to crime. He reported it, and I seemed to keep finding it. Since he'd helped me out a couple of times, there was no reason not to ask for his assistance once again.

"This sounds pretty lame," he said when I finally got hold of him late that afternoon.

"Have I been wrong so far?"

I heard him sigh. "No. Okay, what do you want me to do?"

"See if this guy has paid taxes."

"You got a social security number? Date of birth? Anything like that?"

"According to Facebook, he was born on April

twelfth—no year given."

"And if that's a bogus date?"

"Then I'm shit outta luck."

"You'll be on my shit list, that's for sure." He was quiet for a moment, and I could hear the rustle of paper. "Okay, give me a day or two and I'll get back to you."

He hung up.

A day or two. It was going to seem like years. I just hoped he had things cleared up before my court date or I might find myself in jail—or doing community service. Maybe digging holes in parks for new trees instead of digging in yards looking for bodies.

But I didn't have to wait those two days because Madam Zahara called me. After all, I didn't have an unlisted number and she did know my name.

"Mr. Resnick?" she asked. "The one who visited a psychic on two occasions this past week?"

"That's me," I said as a chill ran up my spine.

"It seems as though we have more business to conduct."

"How so?" I asked.

"You want to know about Fred Butterfield, right?"

"Yes," I said.

"I'm prepared to tell all. And if you want to call the police after you've heard my story, I won't try to stop you."

Boy, did that sound like a trap, or what? But she had me pegged and I did want to hear her story.

"I'm not prepared to go back to the house on Main Street. Can we meet on neutral ground?"

The connection was silent for long seconds. "I'm open to that. Where?"

Someplace crowded. "How about Eastern Hills Mall?"

"Where will we meet?"

"By the food court. Tomorrow afternoon. Is five thirty all right with you?"

"Perfect," she said. She sounded smug, which made the hairs on the back of my neck bristle.

"I'll see you then," I said.

"Damn right you will," she answered and hung up.

I was antsy at work all the next day, watching the clock and messing up drink orders. My boss is pretty forgiving and just chalked it up to me having a bad day. I was worried that the bad element was yet to come. I still wasn't sure what I had gotten myself into, but meeting Madam Zahara in a public place was the prudent thing to do.

I arrived at the mall's food court fifteen minutes before the agreed-upon time. Madam Zahara was already seated at a table near Subway, fidgeting. She was dressed in the same outfit I'd seen her in two days before. She adjusted her shawl, glanced around, and adjusted it again, looking decidedly nervous.

I scoped out the place, didn't see anyone who looked like a long-distance trucker hanging around, and walked up to her table. "Mind if I sit down?"

She waved a hand at the chair opposite her.

I sat down and folded my hands on the table before me. "You called me," I reminded her.

She sighed and leaned closer, keeping her voice low. "First, let me apologize. I shouldn't have taken any money from you, but old habits die hard." She reached into her skirt pocket and withdrew the ten spot and the ones I'd given her the previous times we'd met. She pushed the bills across the table, her bracelets rattling at the movement.

"Any other old habits you'd like to disavow yourself from?" I asked.

She ignored my question, studied my face, and finally spoke. "You were right. There was a horrific murder in my house."

"Fred Butterfield's house," I reminded her.

"It didn't always belong to him."

"Are you saying he bought it from you?"

"Cheated me out of it, more like."

"How?"

She sighed. "A phony marriage license. We were never legally married."

"How long ago was that?"

"The years aren't important. In fact, now they mean nothing."

Maybe not to her . . . .

Her mouth drooped. She reached into her pocket once more and withdrew a slip of paper, which she set on the table. On it was written a name: Gary Madison.

"Who's this?"

"Our son."

I'd never had a kid with her, so I assumed she meant Butterfield. "Is this the long-distance truck driver?"

She nodded. "I was hoping you might try to get a message to him from me. Despite all my best efforts, I haven't been able to contact him."

"What makes you think I can?"

She laughed. "Mr. Resnick, we both know what you are."

"And what's that?"

"Somebody like me. A psychic. Only you're much better than I ever was."

"It wasn't just a game?"

She shook her head. "Reading the Tarot, consulting the crystal—that kept us off welfare and put food on the table while Fred drove around in that money hole of a Corvette."

"I take it he no longer owns it?"

She shook her head. "It's just a reminder of his so-called glory days. He never worried about supporting us."

"Mrs. Butterfield—"

Again she shook her head. "I never took his name."

"I can't say I feel comfortable calling you Madam Zahara."

"My name is Bridget Madison."

I nodded. "Bridget. Where can I find the body?"

"As I'm sure you surmised, in the side yard where the policeman found you the other night. You were so close, too."

"Yeah, well, I can hardly go digging there if you're going to call the cops every time I show up."

"Who says I called the cops?"

"Who else could it have been?" I asked.

"Who do you think?" She looked at me as if I was dense, and yet she was the one talking in circles.

"If I'm going to be taken seriously, I need proof to take to the police."

"I know, I know." She toyed with one of the rings on her fingers. "If you show up at the house later tonight, you'll have your proof."

"You wanna tell me what I'll be up against?"

"And scare you away?" She shook her head. "Now, about that message to my son . . . ."

"Where am I supposed to find him?"

"He's around, and I suspect you wouldn't have much trouble locating him. His birth date and social security number are on the other side of that piece of paper."

I picked it up. Sure enough, the information was there.

She got up from the table. "I hope you'll come by the house to see me later."

"I'll be there."

She nodded, and stood. Her skirt was much longer than I'd thought, and as I watched her move away from the food court, a terrible chill came over me.

Under the filmy fabric, no feet touched the tile floor.

"Okay, now I'm totally confused," Richard said, and got up from the kitchen table to pour himself another glass of scotch. "Are you saying *she's* the ghost?"

"Can ghosts even show up in the middle of the day?" Brenda asked.

"They must. Because I'm telling you, whatever it was I saw had no legs and yet it glided right out of the food court. By the time I got over the shock and hurried after her, she was— *poof!*—gone.

"So it's her body that's buried beside that creepy old house?" Richard asked.

"That's what I'm thinking."

"But didn't you say Fred Butterfield disintegrated right before your eyes?"

"Maybe they're both dead," Brenda suggested, and cut a piece off the medium-rare steak on her plate.

"Somebody ordered a pizza the other night. Somebody called the cops on us, too. And somebody is updating Fred Butterfield's Facebook page."

Richard took his seat once more. "What about the son she wanted you to contact? Could it be him living in the house?"

"Maybe."

"Do you think he killed both of them?"

"What was it she wanted you to tell him?" Brenda asked.

"That's the thing. She never got around to saying it. She just said she hadn't been able to contact him."

"And what will you say if you do find him?" Richard asked. "'Hi. Did you kill your parents?'"

I wasn't sure how to answer. "I think I'd better get on the computer and start looking for him."

Richard shook his head. "No. If he killed his parents, you should go to the police."

"And how serious are they going to take me when I tell them I've seen two ghosts?"

"Can't your friend Sam write a story on the house or something?" Brenda suggested.

"I already called him about it."

"And?" Richard prompted.

I shrugged. "So far nothing."

"Then it might be time to start nagging, because no way do I want you to confront someone who might've killed his mama and daddy," Brenda said.

"Yes, ma'am," I muttered.

Brenda glared at me. "Don't you 'yes, ma'am' me like that. You listen to me."

"Yeah, listen to her," Richard echoed. I was beginning to feel like I was being bullied. The fact that I knew they truly cared about my welfare kind of took the sting out of it, though.

Calling Sam was a good idea. And I had Gary Madison's social security number, so that would make tracking him down a lot easier. If it was correct. I mean, did ghosts usually go around carrying their offspring's social security numbers? And how did a ghost write it down on a piece of paper? Could they hold pens and pencils?

I didn't want to think about it.

After dinner, I went back up to my apartment and called Sam at home. He wasn't exactly thrilled to hear from me so soon.

"Sorry, I've been busy at work—I didn't get a chance to look up that Butterworth guy."

"Butterfield," I corrected. "Mrs. Butterworth is syrup."

"Butterfield, Butterworth," he muttered.

"The story has taken on a new angle. I suspected the psychic to be the killer? Now it looks like she's dead, too."

"Oh my god. Someone killed her? Have you reported this to the cops?"

"No. She's been dead for a long time . . . I think."

"What a minute. She's a ghost, too?" Sam said, sounding incredulous.

"Yeah, but she asked me to track down and contact her son and she gave me his social security number to make it easier."

"Don't all ghosts do that?" he asked sarcastically.

"You could save me a lot of time by corking that number into one of your databases."

"Okay. Let me fire up the computer and I'll do it now."

I had to wait a few minutes for Sam's computer to boot up, but the next thing I knew he was asking me for the number. I heard him tapping his keyboard and anxiously waited for him to report what he found.

"Hmm."

"What does 'hmm' mean?" I asked.

"The guy lives in Portland, Oregon. I've got a phone number." I already had a pen and paper out ready to take any information he had. I wrote it down, plus the address.

"He is listed as a truck driver for RDC Equipment Supply. Looks like it's based in Portland."

"He could still be a long-distance trucker," I said.

"Or maybe he got a new job since the deaths of his parents."

"Oregon's a long way from Western New York," I agreed. "Is there any other information? Mother's name—father's name?"

"No father listed. Mother's name Bridget Madison."

"That's the name the fortuneteller gave me, all right."

"What are you going to do now?"

"Call the number, talk to the guy."

"And if he's uncooperative?"

"Well . . . there's the option of you writing about the house."

"And what angle do I use? Halloween's still more than two months away."

"I might have to go back to the house and dig some more."

"That'll only get you tossed in jail again," Sam pointed out.

"Yeah, by whoever is holed up in that house. But who could it be? Someone's squatting. They've got electric, and they must be paying the taxes on that place."

"Or," Sam said, and drew out the word. "You've imagined all this."

"I didn't imagine the cop that arrested me, or the name the woman gave me, or even the social security number you just looked up."

"Yeah," he agreed. "But something about this whole situation smells fishy to me."

"You and me both."

"Look, I gotta go," Sam said. "Keep me posted."

"Will do," I said with resignation.

I hung up the phone and stared at it. So, he thought I'd imagined all this, huh?

I couldn't have.

I didn't.

Richard had bailed me out of jail, but I had no witnesses for any other part of this whole situation.

I stared at the number I'd written down. If Gary Madison had a day job, it was way too early to call the west coast. I'd have to wait until later in the evening. But what the hell was I going to say? *Know any good ghost stories? Did you know your mother's a ghost?* Or how about, *Halloween came early—guess how?*

There was only one thing to do. I stepped up to my liquor cabinet and poured myself a shot of bourbon and hoped I'd figure out something more appropriate to say when the time came.

The eleven o'clock news had just begun with a lead story about a drowning in Lake Erie. I dialed the Portland number that by then I knew by heart, and hit the mute button on my remote control. The Channel 7 newscaster's lips moved as the line rang and rang. Maybe Gary Madison wasn't yet home from work. I had to work the next day and didn't feel like staying up until the wee hours to try calling again. I was just about to hang up when a voice answered, "Hello."

I sat up straighter on the couch. Suddenly my mouth had gone dry. "Uh, Gary Madison? Son of Bridget Madison and Fred Butterfield?"

"Yeah," he answered warily.

"My name is Jeff Resnick. You don't know me . . . but I've got a really weird story to tell you about your parents."

There was dead silence for several long seconds. "Yeah," he said finally.

"I've been to their old house on Route 5, and I had a really odd experience."

I heard him sigh, as though he was already bored by my tale.

"I've . . . I've seen them—talked to them both."

He sighed once more and said, "Not again."

"I beg your pardon?"

"There's a reason I left Buffalo, Mister . . . what did you say your name was?"

"Resnick. Jeff Resnick."

"There's a reason I left Buffalo, Jeff. To get away from my parents. Now I know every kid eventually says that, but they don't have to say it after their parents are dead."

"You've seen them since they passed?"

"Let me guess. My mother asked you to track me down. Even gave you my social security number, I'll bet."

"That she did."

"Did she make you think that a murder had taken

place in the house?"

"Yeah. Was she murdered?"

"Only by cigarettes and vodka. I'd call that death by suicide."

"How about your father?"

"Fell down the stairs after a few too many beers. Broke his neck. That was fifteen years ago."

Damn. I should've checked the county records for a death certificate. "He's got a Facebook page."

"No, I've got a Facebook page and I post as him."

"Why?"

"Because that way I can find out what's going on with my friends in Buffalo without my ex-wife harassing me."

That made sense. Still . . . . "How long ago did your mother pass?"

"Four years."

Which explained why Butterfield looked so much younger than Madam Zahara.

"But I don't get it. Dead is dead. Why are they still in that house? What's keeping your parents from . . . moving on?"

"Probably pure spite. I mean, they sure got under your skin, and let me tell you, you aren't the first who's called me about this situation. I talked to a priest about exorcism, but he blew me off. It probably wouldn't have worked, anyway. They didn't respect the church in life, why give a shit about it in death?"

"I sensed there might be bodies buried in the side yard."

"It's where their ashes were scattered. It was a lot cheaper than buying a couple of cemetery plots," Madison explained.

So much for him being a loving son.

"Is there someone living in the house now?" I asked.

"Yeah, my cousin is there. I'm letting him stay there until the sale is final."

So that's who owned the Buick. "There's no sign up in front."

"Yeah, my real estate agent complained they kept disappearing. I figured it was either my cousin or my dad ripping them down. A developer has bought most of the property on that stretch of the road for senior living units. They'll take possession of the place on the first of the month. I figure caveat emptor. Razing the house should finally get mom and dad out of my hair forever."

No love lost among those three.

"I found an ad on the online white pages for Madam Zahara's psychic services."

"The Internet is forever," he said.

That was the truth. "Have you told them the house is coming down?"

"Nope."

"What about your cousin?"

"I told him to be out by the end of the week. He's resisting. I figure I'll tell him why closer to the date of the sale. I don't want him slipping up and saying something to warn mom and dad."

Somebody should.

"I'm sorry you got suckered into this," Madison said. "It shouldn't happen anymore once the house is gone."

The restless spirits of his parents might not just be tied to the house, but attached to land it stood on, too.

Caveat emptor indeed.

"Thanks for speaking with me. I won't bother you again."

"And don't let my folks bother you, either," Madison warned.

"Thanks."

I hung up the phone.

Bridget Madison and Fred Butterfield might not have been the nicest people when they were alive, but did they deserve what their son had in store for them?

I had a feeling I should keep my nose out of this situation . . . but I was pissed at them for jerking me around, and determined to make one more visit to that dilapidated house on Route 5.

I put in another day of work at The Whole Nine Yards, but instead of heading home, I turned right and headed back to Clarence. Sure enough, the neon sign proclaiming Psychic $10 was once again glowing. Apparently just marks like me could see it. Did Madison's cousin ever wonder about the people traipsing in and out of his temporary home, or was he just as oblivious about us as he was about the home's permanent residents?

I parked my car on the gravel drive and walked up to the house. Once again Bridget called out, "I've been waiting for you." No doubt she had been.

I opened the screen door and walked inside the house. The black floor greeted me once again. I crouched down to better inspect it. It sure looked like old water damage to me.

"What are you waiting for?" Bridget called.

I straightened and headed into the parlor where she sat behind the table once again.

"I talked to your son," I said, not waiting for her to ask.

Her eyes lit up. "And, and?" she asked, sounding pleased.

"He's sold the house."

Her expression fell. "He can't do that!"

I shrugged. "He already has. Your upstairs tenant doesn't even know. He's just been told to get out by the end of the week."

"No wonder he's been packing," Bridget said angrily.

I looked up. Fred Butterfield was again standing at the side of the room. He looked grim.

"Not only that, but as soon as the sale is final, a bull-dozer will be here to knock the house down."

Bridget shot Butterfield an angry glare. "Did you hear what Mr. Resnick said?"

Butterfield nodded, looking worried.

"Where will we go?"

"Maybe it's time for you to move on?" I suggested.

She turned her head to face me. "To what? Oblivion?"

"Isn't that what we're all supposed to do . . . eventually?"

"Well, I'm not ready," she declared. She looked over her shoulder toward her common-law husband. "Are you?"

Butterfield looked resigned. He shrugged.

Bridget looked back to me. "Will Gary at least come back to see us one more time?" Her voice was a plea.

I shook my head.

Bridget's face screwed into a grimace and she burst into tears.

I had never seen a ghost cry before.

What the hell was I thinking? Until I'd met these two, I'd never seen a ghost before. I still wasn't sure what I was seeing was real. I could just be imaging all of this.

No I wasn't. I'd been arrested. I'd seen Bridget walk with no legs. I'd talked to Gary Madison. This was the real deal and if I hadn't already had a bunch of weird experiences I'd just say I was crazy.

Still, seeing a ghost cry was just plain weird, and yet I couldn't ignore the emotional turmoil going on in front of me.

"I'm sorry," I said at last.

I looked at Butterfield, who once again shrugged. Then he stepped over to Bridget and pulled her hands away from her face.

"You're leaving, aren't you?" she asked.

He frowned and nodded.

"But then I'll be all alone."

"Not if you come with me," he said. I hadn't heard him speak before, and his voice was a lot higher than I'd anticipated.

"But Gary—

"Doesn't care."

Bridget's lower lip started to tremble. "But—"

"Besides, I'm bored hanging around here all the time. I'm ready to blow this pop stand and see what else is out there. Wanna come with me?"

Bridget's face was filled with indecision.

"Once this house is gone . . . there'll be nothing for us here anyway. Come on," he urged. "I'm ready for a new adventure. Let's go." He pulled her up from the chair. They stood there, or should I say Bridget hovered—she still didn't seem to have feet—and they looked into each other's eyes for a long, long time. And then they just . . . dissolved into nothingness.

I blinked and the room was different. The card table and its contents were gone. My nose wrinkled at the smell of moldering food, and the breeze rustled the fast food papers that littered the floor. Was Madison's cousin upstairs? If so, I didn't want to run into him I got the hell out of that house as fast as I could. Gravel flew as I backed out of the drive and headed for home, clenching the steering wheel the whole distance.

Holy shit. There really were ghosts.

And I'd spoken to two of them.

For the next couple of weeks, every time I'd visit Maggie, I took the back route. It was about a month later when I finally gathered up my courage to drive by the house I'd come to think of as ghost central. Of course, it was gone. So were the trees. All that was left was level ground and a sign that said Donard Construction and Fine Senior Living at Donard Estates.

I will admit that I checked Fred Butterfield's Facebook page on a regular basis. As Gary had said, he kept it going, and presumably without a twinge of conscience. He had said his parents were con artists. I was their last mark. That they couldn't pull any more shenanigans was all for the best.

That is . . . if they were done conning people.

The last time I drove by it was night, and when I looked to the empty spot where the house had been, I almost swear I saw the outline of a woman with a filmy skirt and shawl smoking a cigarette.

Of course . . . I could have just imagined it.

It's Christmas Day, and Richard and Brenda are off to warmer climes, leaving Jeff and Maggie to spend Christmas dinner with Maggie's famiy. But the Brennan clan has not rolled out the welcome mat for Jeff. It'll be a Christmas to remember ... but who wants to?

Bah, Humbug

"You won't forget to top up the water in the Christmas tree stand, will you?" my brother Richard asked, his gaze darting to the long line at the security check-in outside the waiting area at the Buffalo Niagara International Airport.

"No," I told him for the tenth time. And I wouldn't forget to water the plants, clear off the steps, or do any of the other nit-picky chores he'd outlined on the list he'd left taped to his refrigerator door.

"We should've gotten an artificial tree. Then I wouldn't have had to worry..." he went on.

"You'd worry if we'd gotten a flame-retardant, stainless steel tree with sprinklers connected to every branch," his wife Brenda piped up, as she stooped to rearrange the top layer of books, candy, vitamins, and other sundries in her carry-on bag. Brenda never traveled light.

"Just think, later tonight you'll be standing on a beach, under romantic moonlight," my girlfriend Maggie said and sighed.

"If the plane isn't late. Or the weather acts up, or—"

"Will you stop being so pessimistic," Brenda told Richard.

"I don't know why I'm so nervous," he admitted, and tugged at the collar of his turtleneck shirt. No wonder he was sweating. He also had on a parka—something he wouldn't be needing south of the border.

"I'm the one who gets premonitions," I told him. It

had been that way since March, when I'd been bashed in the head with a baseball bat by some punk who thought he needed my wallet more than I did. Since then I'd known a lot of things—and not many of them were pleasant. Brenda says I'm psychic. I say ... I know *some* things. "I predict you guys will have a wonderful, relaxing, stress-free vacation."

"That's good enough for me," Brenda said, and snatched up Richard's hand, squeezing it.

He managed a hesitant smile, the edges of his mustache quirking upward.

A family of five, all loaded down with carry-on baggage, passed us, and the line at security got that much longer. "We'd better get going," Brenda said, noticing. She captured Maggie in a hug. "Now take care of Jeffy while we're gone. Make sure he eats at least one good meal a day."

"I will, I will," Maggie promised.

Brenda grabbed me next, kissing me on the cheek. "And take care of my girlfriend."

"You'll only be gone six days. How much trouble can either of us get into?"

Brenda pulled away, giving me the fish eye. "Knowing you, a lot!"

"Come on," Richard urged, picking up their carry-on luggage. He paused, giving me a knowing look that transcended words. A look that said, "I love you. I'm glad you're back in my life. And don't forget to take out the trash," all rolled into one. I hoped he read most of the same on my face. What he actually said was, "Take care of the house, kid. I'm depending on you."

"Be good," Brenda called, following Richard to the waiting line. "Merry Christmas!"

"Bon voyage!" Maggie wrapped one arm around mine, waving to their backs as they joined the line of sheep waiting for the dreaded security nightmare that preceded all flights.

We turned to walk toward the terminal's exit, and I swallowed down the lump that had formed in my throat. The best part of my holiday had just ended.

"I wish it was like the old days when you could stay in the waiting area and wave to the plane as it took off," Maggie said, wistfully.

"Me, too." Maybe then I wouldn't feel quite so abandoned?

Maggie's crystal blue eyes were moist with understanding. "The good old days," she whispered, and her hand snaked down to take mine. All around us, the airport hummed with passengers and visitors, tearful goodbyes and joyful hellos. It was painful to experience and I wanted to get the hell out of there. I picked up my pace, dragging Maggie along with me.

"I wish we were going with them," she said.

"They need time alone. Time to heal."

She nodded, no doubt thinking about the trauma we'd all endured earlier in the month, thanks to Ray Sampson.

"I've had a good day," Maggie said, fingering the garnet pendant on the chain around her neck. I'd bought it for her, not considering she might wear a red sweater for Christmas. It couldn't compare with the diamond solitaire earrings Richard had given Brenda. Or the emerald necklace, or the sapphire ring ... the trip to Mexico, and ....

"Me, too."

It had been the best Christmas of my life, but I had this funny feeling the day wouldn't end on such a happy note.

Maybe I did wish I could've gotten on that plane.

We headed for the short-term parking lot. Maybe we should have said our goodbyes outside the terminal, but Maggie and I had time to kill, and I wasn't quite ready to let the best Christmas I'd ever had end.

To say the air was bracing was putting it mildly, though late afternoon sunlight glinted off the parked cars as I huddled into my jacket and lowered my head so as not to take a direct hit from the wind. Unless the plane hit clear-air turbulence, they had perfect flying weather.

We claimed Richard's Lincoln Town Car, paid the parking fee, and started off for Lackawanna and the Brennan family Christmas gathering.

Bah, humbug.

Except for carols on the radio, the drive was a quiet one. Even Maggie's usually buoyant enthusiasm had flattened into nothingness as clouds began to gather in the west.

"It'll be fine," Maggie said at last.

I gave her a skeptical glance, but said nothing. She didn't have that familiar quiver in her gut, a feeling I'd learned to be wary of. She didn't have that niggling itch in the back of her skull—trouble on the way. Only I didn't know what kind of trouble. And for all her soothing words, she was worried about something and had been transmitting it for the past hour.

We pulled up the driveway and I cut the engine.

The handmade wreath on the front door was heavy with what looked like real fruit, straight out of a Colonial Williamsburg brochure. Maggie's sister Irene's deft hand, no doubt. According to Maggie, Irene made sure everything about her home, her children, and her marriage was perfect. Or else.

That's probably why she didn't like me. Not only was I flawed, but I was essentially broke. And I was ruining her sister's life. Not that she'd said so the one time I'd met her back in September. That was after the accident that totaled my car. I wasn't hurt, but Maggie.... Well, the five-inch scar on her right calf might fade in another couple of years. Considering she'd nearly bled to death, that wasn't too bad a price to pay.

I opened the trunk and retrieved the brightly wrapped presents, then followed Maggie up the walk. She pressed the doorbell and we waited. Minuscule snowflakes gently landed in Maggie's auburn hair. She smiled and impulsively kissed me.

The door flew open and Irene, dressed in a gold sequined top, dark silk pants, with perfectly coiffed hair the color of muslin and carefully applied make-up, stood before us. "Maggie, darling," she cried, and gathered her sister in a careful hug. She glanced at me over Maggie's shoulder. Her smile faded.

"Jeff," she said coolly.

"Irene."

I stood there with my arms laden with packages Maggie had insisted on adding my name to. But I didn't know these people, hadn't contributed toward the cost of the gifts.

Irene ushered us into her tastefully decorated Colonial home, to the formal living room where Maggie's kin were sitting on the stiff, uncomfortable-looking furniture. Irene took our coats, and Maggie and I added the pile of gifts to the overflowing stack under the Christmas tree. It was Brennan family custom to open presents after dinner, she'd told me.

The holiday spirit seemed in short supply, although the adults were all sipping drinks. The kids were off in another part of the house, whooping and hollering, which gave the only hint of holiday cheer. As I took in the somber faces around me, a sensation of smothering concern for Maggie seeped into me. It permeated the room.

It would be a long evening.

"Can I get you anything?" a vaguely familiar face politely asked.

"Jeff, you remember Irene's husband, Peter," Maggie said.

"Peter," I said in acknowledgment. The painless dentist, and the source of status Irene so coveted. "Bourbon on the rocks, please."

"Maggie?"

"White wine would be great," she said, and Peter turned for the makeshift bar in the corner. Moments later, we collected our drinks.

"Let me introduce you around," Maggie said, and turned toward the couple sitting in the love seat. "You remember my sister Sandy and her husband Dave."

They nodded. Dave didn't offer his hand. Just as well. I didn't want to touch him. Or anyone else. That might kick-start my sixth sense that let me know what people were feeling—and sometimes even thinking. But touching any of them didn't seem like it would be a problem tonight. I'd been branded a pariah.

As I was introduced around the room, I knew the dark feelings I experienced were more than my own paranoia. Maggie's family had already made up their minds to dislike me. But why?

Irene returned with a tray full of stuffed mushroom caps. She offered them to everyone. Everyone but me.

Okay.

Taking the chair farthest from the group, I looked for something to distract myself. The shelves against the back wall were full of bric-a-brac, but not a magazine or a book graced the tables—not even the morning's newspaper.

I nursed my bourbon. This was as bad as sitting in a hospital waiting room. Okay, I knew that routine for killing time. Two times two is four. Three times two is six. Four times two is eight....

I made it to the sixes before Maggie caught up on the latest family gossip and found me.

"You okay?" she asked.

I could've told her I had a migraine, that I needed to go home. But why ruin her Christmas with her family because I was uncomfortable with them? Besides, something in my gut told me we ought to stay. That was good enough for me.

"I'm fine."

"You're awfully quiet."

I shrugged. "I don't do well with new people."

"So mingle," she said and smiled.

God, I loved her. She wanted her family to like me. She knew they didn't. Did she know why?

I decided to push it. "Is something going on I should know about?"

Maggie's smile waned.

"Maggs?" I pressed.

"I don't know," she admitted, her expression darkening, her gaze darting to the crowd in front of the fireplace. "But I don't like it. I'll tell Irene—"

"No, don't say anything. It's not worth it."

"But you're important to me. I don't want them to—"

I touched her arm. "Maggs, it's just for a couple of hours. I'll hang back and keep a low profile"

"But you shouldn't have to." Her whisper was turning harsh.

"Can I get you another drink?" Peter asked from behind her.

I peered around Maggie. "No, thanks, I'm fine."

Peter nodded and went back to his other guests.

Maggie's cheeks flushed pink as she blinked back tears.

"Babe, just go be with your family. I'm fine. It'll be okay."

"But, you're part of my family now, too."

I gave her a smile. "Thanks." She took a breath and forced a smile.

"Go," I told her and kissed her nose.

"I love you," she said, and kissed me back.

She turned and moved to stand next to her sister

Sandy, who was talking to their mother.

I couldn't take my eyes off Maggie. We're good for one another. She kept my mind off other things—and people—who were off limits. Somehow we'd get through this evening, and later make love, and then I'd show her just how much she meant to me.

A grandfather clock near the archway to the dining room chimed five. Dinner wouldn't be served for another hour. I edged around the two tables Irene had set in the dining room; one for the adults and one for the children. The silverware had been polished until it glowed. Sparking crystal, starched and folded linen napkins, and calligraphied name cards graced each setting. Maggie's parents would sit in the places of honor at the head of the table. Maggie and I were halfway down, with my chair smack against a leg of the table. I'd have to straddle it the whole meal.

Since no one was paying attention to me anyway, I wandered off in search of the kids.

The large-screen plasma TV in the family room was alive with pint-sized warriors doing battle. Two teenaged boys sat behind controllers manipulating the televised titans. They didn't acknowledge my presence, but since few of their parents had either, I didn't take it personally.

A couple of smaller boys played with toy cars on the rug. They muttered a subdued "hi," and crashed miniature NASCAR racers into the furniture and baseboards.

The lone female had her nose buried in a book. I stood next to the couch, watching the game in progress. The girl's gaze slid over the top of the book.

"You're aunt Maggie's lover, aren't you?"

I wasn't sure how to answer that. "She's my girlfriend. What's your name?"

"Eleanor."

God, I thought that name went out with First Lady Roosevelt.

"Hi, Eleanor. I'm Jeff."

"Are you a millionaire?" this teenaged-Irene clone asked.

I laughed. "I'm not even a thousandaire."

She wasn't amused. "That's what I thought." She eyed my sweater and slacks, her gaze lingering for a moment on my crotch. "But you've got millionaires in your family, right?"

Funny how that little piece of news always precedes me. "Just one."

"A brother, right?"

"Yeah."

What else did this nosy kid know about me?

"How come you're not rich?" she persisted.

"The luck of the draw." I drained my glass and went off in search of a refill.

Peter wasn't hovering around his minibar, so I decided to serve myself. Irene glanced up at me from her post holding up the fireplace. Peter was quietly conversing with the family patriarch when Irene nudged him. What did she think I'd do, steal her crystal?

Peter crossed the room. "What can I get you, Jeff?"

"Another bourbon, thanks."

Peter lifted the lid on the ice bucket, found it empty. "Damn."

"Honey, the fire needs banking," Irene said.

"I can get more ice. Freezer, right?"

"The kitchen's through there." Peter handed me the ice bucket.

The tension eased as soon as the swinging door closed behind me. Away from the blast of the fire, the cool kitchen was a welcome relief. The glossy granite counters were clear of food prep. There was no heavenly aroma of roasting turkey--not even a potato boiled on the stove. We must be waiting for the caterer to arrive.

I opened the freezer, poking at the seven-pound bag

of ice.

"What're you doing in my freezer?" asked a cold voice.

I turned, showed Irene the ice bucket in my hand. "Peter asked me to fill it."

Irene crossed the kitchen in four steps and snatched it from me. I stepped back as she took tongs from a drawer and opened the freezer door. "I understand you're Jewish," she said with a sneer, extracting ice from the plastic bag.

"My father was Jewish. I was raised a Catholic."

"That still makes you half Jewish."

"That doesn't make me anything."

Her lips curled in contempt. "You're right. You're nothing."

The hairs on the back of my neck bristled. How could this dreadful, tactless, bigoted woman be related to my sweet loving Maggie? And what did she think of Maggie's best—black—friend, Brenda?

"Why did you invite me here, since you obviously don't like me?"

"For Maggie, of course," she said, practically throwing ice into the bucket.

Yes. Maggie. And I supposed I could suffer for a little while longer. At least until Maggie had had enough.

"My sister led a calm, safe life until the day you barged into it. First, her boss was murdered—"

"That happened before I met Maggie."

"She lost her job—"

"That wasn't my fault."

"Your lousy driving nearly killed her."

"We were run off the road."

"Only weeks ago some kook broke into your brother's house and cracked her over the head, giving her a concussion."

No doubt about it, I was a trouble magnet. Maggie

had faced moments of danger and unpleasantness at my side.

"You're not good enough for my sister," she grated, finished filling the bucket and slammed the freezer door. "You'll never amount to anything, and if you were any kind of gentleman, you'd leave her alone and let her get on with her life."

I exhaled angrily. "I love Maggie. I would never do anything to hurt her."

"You're a loser. Now, get out of my kitchen."

I would've liked to have smacked that sneer from her face. Instead, I just glared at her.

The door from the living room swished open. Maggie poked her head inside. "Oh, there you two are. Irene, the caterer's at the front door. Do you want them to set up now?"

"They're early," Irene groused, abandoned the ice bucket, and rushed from the room.

"Did I just miss something?" Maggie asked.

I gave her a smile. "No, babe, everything's okay." I retrieved the now-full ice bucket and followed Maggie back to the living room.

Irene blossomed into the equivalent of a Broadway producer as she directed the catering firm where to place the food. Next she bossed the family to the table, and dutifully every one fell into line like drafted soldiers, taking their seats.

The caterers were dismissed and Irene directed the dissemination of turkey, cranberries, and vegetables. The Brennan clan dished out huge portions of stuffing and all the other accouterments, while I took a small scoop of potatoes, a slice of turkey and a spoonful of stuffing.

I glanced at my watch and figured Richard and Brenda were probably halfway to Cozumel. Brenda had been disappointed when Richard announced he'd booked the trip for Christmas Day. She'd wanted to put on a complete holiday feast, but I'd convinced her that January 6th—Epiphany—could be her last stab at making merry for this holiday season.

The Brennan family weren't great conversationalists, but Irene was asking each in turn how they liked the food. While occupied, their collective disdain for me had diminished, but I still found it weird that they'd taken on Irene's dislike for me as a form of family unity.

I pushed a morsel of stuffing around my plate before forking it into my mouth.

"What's the matter, Jeff, isn't the food good enough for you?" Irene eyed me with scorn.

Well, at least she addressed me by my name and not *Hey, you.* I swallowed. "It's very good. I'm just not a big eater."

"I wish I had your lack of appetite," Maggie said and gave a hollow laugh. "Everything's delicious, Irene." Maggie would've said that even if she was choking on it.

Irene turned her attention to her father and I poked at the mashed potatoes on my plate. Maybe we'd only have to stay another hour. But there was still that mound of gifts to open. Did the Brennan clan open them one-by-one, or did they have a rip-fest with wrapping paper flying and demolish the pile in record speed? I could only hope ....

I took a bite of turkey, chewing slowly when I was hit by a sudden sense of panic emanating from nearby. I swallowed quickly and for a moment the meat caught in my throat. I grabbed my drink and took a gulp, but the panic I felt kicked into high gear.

Someone at the table was choking—couldn't communicate it—and a flame of fear coursed through me.

My gaze darted to those at the table, but everyone seemed to be conversing or fixated with the food on their plates.

Then I knew.

I shoved back my chair with such force that the table shuddered.

"Jeff?" Maggie asked.

I ignored her and stumbled against Peter's chair, shoving him forward and nearly into his plate.

"Hey!"

Like magnetic force, I felt drawn to the kids' table, panic nearly choking me, too.

The smallest boy at the satellite table had placed a hand on his throat. I grabbed him from behind, pulled him off his chair and placed my clenched fist against his sternum and gave a mighty jerk. The boy made croaking sounds, and his panic kicked into overdrive.

I gave him another two quick jerks and a hunk of turkey ejected from his mouth, landing on Eleanor's plate.

"Eeeooooooo!" she wailed, and jumped to her feet. Her plate went flying and crashed against the wall, where it shattered into a dozen pieces.

Irene shot out of her chair like a missile. "What the hell are you doing?" she screamed.

The boy—Brian?—was limp in my arms, coughing, struggling for breath.

"Put that child down," Irene hollered, and launched herself at me.

I dropped the kid back into his seat, but Irene crashed into me, her arms flying—windmill style—slapping at me, shoving me backward.

"You goddamned bastard—you've ruined our Christmas!"

I tried to get around her, but Irene had forty or fifty pounds on me, and I slammed into the buff-painted wall. A framed picture fell, glass shattering as it hit the hardwood floor.

"Mama, Mama!" the little boy wailed.

Peter was suddenly there, yanking his wife off of me,

grabbing her arms and pulling her away.

Sandy had grabbed her son in a fierce hug, patting his back.

"I couldn't breathe, I couldn't breathe!" the boy cried, and buried his face in her sweatered shoulder.

"How did you know?" Sandy asked, her face taut with fear. "You couldn't see the kids from your seat. How did you know?" she demanded.

All eyes were on me. Maggie hadn't told them about my gift. Instead of gratitude, the entire family looked at me with suspicion—as though *I* had caused the kid to choke.

"What *are* you?" Irene asked.

I saw a wild-eyed Maggie standing behind her confused parents. "I've had enough," I told her, and headed for the front door. Grabbing my jacket—from the closet floor—I struggled into the sleeves and yanked open the front door, letting it slam behind me.

I made it to the car by the time Maggie came running after me, sans coat. "Jeff, wait!"

I opened the driver's door, the dome light spilling wan light onto the darkened, snowy drive.

"Where are you going?" Maggie said.

"Where else? Home."

She stood there, hands cupping opposite elbows, shivering in the cold. "I don't think they realize you just saved Brian's life."

"Yeah, well, I don't think I'll hang around to wait for their show of appreciation. Give my regrets to Irene, will you?"

"Jeff, please come back in. I'll explain everything. I'll make them understand."

"You can't. Don't you see, Maggie, Irene has already poisoned them against me. Maybe she's right. Maybe I'm nothing but trouble for you. You might just be better off without me."

"But I think I love you."

That would never be good enough for her close-knit family. With a failed marriage behind her, Maggie already had a blemished record where men were concerned.

"I love you, too, but—" They were never going to accept me, and shoving that fact down her throat on Christmas Day was too cruel for even me to attempt.

"Can someone drive you back to Richard's to pick up your car?"

"I'm coming back with you now."

"No, you're not. That'll just put a bigger wedge between you and your family and I don't want that for you. Sandy and Dave live in Tonawanda, don't they? That's not too far from Richard's house."

"But—"

"Go on. Go back in. Smooth things over. It'll be okay."

But instead of retreating, she shuffled through the inch or so of new snow and threw herself into my arms, swamping me with a tsunami of emotions: love, shame, and pride all rolled together in an almost overwhelming amalgam.

"I'm so ashamed," she sobbed into my shoulder. "How could my family let me down like this?"

"They're just worried about you being with someone like me." And probably with reason.

She held onto me with fierce determination. "I love you," she asserted, and yet this thing inside me that could tap into others' emotions told me she really wasn't sure what she felt. Oh yeah, she felt some kind of affection, but deep down love? No, she just wasn't sure.

And why should she?

I kissed the top of her head, then pushed her away. "You're shivering. Go back inside. If you want to come back to my place later, I'll wait for you. If not ... that's okay, too."

"I'll be there. You can't keep me away."

Yeah, but how much longer would she feel that way? Irene held much more influence over her than Maggie realized. I pulled her close again, hoped I imparted some of my warmth. "I love you, Maggs."

"I love you, too."

She didn't. Yet. Maybe never. But that was okay. I could accept it.

At least for now.

Cold Case . . . the short story that inspired the 5th Jeff Resnick mystery, BOUND BY SUGGESTION.

Psychic Jeff Resnick has no expectations when investigating the disappearance of a four-year-old boy. That is until he confronts the mind responsible--a shattering experience for all involved.

COLD CASE

"You're not the first psychic to come through Paula's apartment, Mr. Resnick."

Hands on hips, Dr. Krista Marsh stood before me. Her heels gave her an inch or more on me. Blonde and lithe, and clad in a turquoise dress with jet beads resting on her ample breasts, she was the best looking thing in that lower middle-class apartment.

"I don't use that term. Con-artists, liars, and frauds take advantage of people with problems. I'm just someone who sometimes knows more than I'm comfortable knowing."

Truth was, I hadn't wanted to be there at all, giving my impressions on the fate of four-year-old Eric Devlin. He'd gone missing on an early-autumn evening some eight months before. One minute he'd been there—riding his Big Wheel in front of the apartment building—the next he was gone. Like every other good citizen, I'd read all the stories in the newspapers and seen the kid's picture on posters and on TV. The only place I hadn't seen it was on the back of a milk carton.

I was there as a favor to my brother—actually, my older half-brother—Dr. Richard Alpert, who'd joined me on that cold gray evening in early May. Richard was Paula Devlin's internist at the university's low-income clinic. He liked Paula and hated how not knowing her son's fate was tearing her apart. He hoped I could shed some light on the kid's disappearance.

I'm not sure why Dr. Marsh was there. Maybe as Paula's therapist she thought she could protect her patient from someone like me.

So, there I stood, in the middle of Paula's modestly furnished living room, trying to soak up vibes that might tell me the little boy's fate.

Paula waited in the doorway, looking fearful as I examined the heart of her home, which she'd transformed into a cottage industry, distributing posters, pins, and flyers in the search for the boy—all to no avail. Vacuum cleaner tracks on the carpet showed her hasty clean-up prior to our arrival. Too thin, and looking older than her thirty-two years, Paula's spirit and her determination to find her missing son had sustained her over the long months she'd been alone. The paper had never mentioned a Mr. Devlin.

"I don't know if I can help you," I told Paula.

She flashed an anxious look at Richard, then back to me.

"Where would you like to start, Mr. Resnick?"

"Call me Jeff. How about Eric's room?"

A sixty-watt bulb illuminated the gloom as the four of us trudged down a narrow hallway. Paula opened the door to a small bedroom, flipped a light switch, and ushered us in. "It's just the way he left it."

I doubted that, since the bed was made and all the toys and games were neatly stacked on shelves under the room's only window—not a speck of dust. A race car bedspread and matching drapes gave a clue to the boy's chief interest—so did the scores of dented, paint-scraped cars and trucks. I picked up a purple-and-black dune buggy, sensing a trace of the boy's aura. He'd been a rambunctious kid, with the beginnings of a smart mouth.

"He was a very lively child."

"He's all boy, that's for sure," his mother said proudly.

She hadn't noticed I'd used the past tense. Either that or she was in deep denial. I'd known little Eric was dead the moment I entered the apartment.

I gave her a half-hearted smile, replaced the toy on the shelf. There wasn't much else to see. I shouldered my way past the others and wandered back to the living room. They tried not to bump into each other as they followed.

A four-foot poster of Eric's smiling face dominated the west wall. He'd been small for his age, cute, with sandy hair and a sprinkle of freckles across the bridge of his nose.

An image flashed through my mind: a child's hand reaching for a glass.

I hitched in a breath, grateful my back was to Dr. Marsh. A mix of powerful emotions erupted—as though my presence had ignited an emotional powder keg. Like repelling magnets, guilt and relief waged a war, practically raining from the walls and ceiling.

Composing myself, I turned, a disquieting depression settling over me.

"Ms. Devlin—"

She stepped forward. "Call me Paula."

"Paula. Did Dr. Alpert tell you how this works?"

"He said you absorb emotions, interpret them, and that sometimes you get knowledge."

"That's right." More or less. "There's a lot of background emotion here. May I hold your hand for a moment? I need to see if it's coming from you, or if it's resident in the building."

Without hesitation, she held out her hand, her expression full of hope. And that's what I got from her: Hope, desperation, and deep despair. She loved that little boy, heart and soul. And there was suspicion, too, but not of me.

I released her hand, letting out the breath I hadn't realized I'd been holding.

"Paula, ever heard the expression about a person taking up all the air in the room?" Her brows puckered in confusion. "You're broadcasting so many emotions I can't sort them out. I know you want to stay, but I can't do what I have to if you're here."

"But he's my son," she protested.

Dr. Marsh stepped closer, placed a comforting hand on Paula's shoulder. "You want him to give you a true reading."

I turned on the psychiatrist. "I'm not a fortune teller, Dr. Marsh."

"I didn't mean to offend," she said without sincerity.

"I'll go if you say so, Krista." Paula grabbed her windbreaker from the closet and headed for the door. Once she was gone, my anxiety eased, and I no longer needed to play diplomat.

"What're you getting?" Richard asked.

"The kid's dead—been dead since day one. He wasn't frightened either, not until the very last minute."

"You're talking murder," Richard said. "Not Paula."

"No. I'm sure of that."

Dr. Marsh eyed me critically, brows arched, voice coolly professional. "Are you well acquainted with sensing death, Mr. Resnick?"

"More than I'd like." I glanced at Richard. "What's this about a pervert in the neighborhood?"

His eyes narrowed. "It hasn't been reported in the media, but Paula told me about the cops' prime suspect. A convicted pedophile lived three units down at the time the boy disappeared. They've had him in for questioning five or six times but haven't been able to wring a confession out of him. How'd you know?"

"From Paula—just now. She's afraid he took her kid."

Dr. Marsh frowned. She probably figured I was just

some shyster running a con. Can't say I was sorry to disappoint her.

"You got something else," Richard said. He knew me well.

"I saw something, but it doesn't make sense." I told them about the vision.

"Close your eyes. Focus on it," he directed.

I shot a look at Dr. Marsh, saw the contempt in her gaze. Skepticism came with the territory.

My eyes slid shut and I allowed myself to relax, trying to relive that fleeting moment.

"What do you see?" Richard said.

"A kid's hand reached for a glass."

"Is it Eric?"

"I don't know."

"Describe the glass."

I squeezed my eyes tighter, trying to replay the image. "A clear tumbler."

"What's inside?"

"Liquid. Brown. Chocolate milk?"

"Look up the child's arm," Richard directed. "Can you see his clothes?"

The cuff of a sleeve came into focus. "Yeah."

"The color?"

I exhaled a breath. Like a camera pulling back, the vision expanded to include the child's chest. "Blue...a decal of—" The image winked out. "Damn!"

"Give it a couple of minutes and try again," Richard advised.

Uncomfortable under Dr. Marsh's stare, I wandered into the kitchen again. I couldn't shake the feeling of...dread? Whatever it was surrounded me, squeezing my chest so I couldn't take a decent breath.

Hands clenched at his side, Richard studied me in silence. We'd been through this before, and his eyes mirrored the concern he wouldn't express for fear of embarrassing me. He knew just what these little empathic forays cost me.

Turning away from his scrutiny, I went back into the boy's gloomy bedroom. Though banished from the apartment, Paula's anguish was still palpable. How many times had she stood in that doorway and cried for her child?

I ran my hands along all the surfaces a kid Eric's age could've touched. After eight months there was so little left of him. His clothes in the dresser drawers, neatly folded and stacked, bore no trace of his aura. I pulled back the bedspread, picked up the pillow, closed my eyes and pressed it against my face. Tendrils of fear curled through me.

Airless.

Darkness.

Nothingness.

Death.

A rustling noise at the open doorway broke the spell. Dr. Marsh studied me as she must've once looked at rats in a lab. Her appraising gaze was sharp, her irritation almost palpable. Even so, she looked like she just walked off the set of some TV drama instead of the University's Medical Center campus. I'd bet her brown eyes flashed when she smiled. Not that she had.

"I understand you've done this before," she said.

"Define 'this,'" I said.

"Helping the police in murder investigations."

"Once or twice."

"Are you always successful?"

"So far," I answered honestly and replaced the pillow, smoothing the spread back into place.

"And what do you get out of it?"

Her scornful tone annoyed me.

"Usually a miserable headache. What is this, an interrogation?"

"I'm merely curious," she said. "My, we are defensive,

aren't we?"

"I can't answer for 'we,' but I'm certainly not here to fence with you, doctor. If you'll excuse me."

Brushing past her, I headed back to the kitchen. The smooth walls and ceiling were practically vibrating. Eric's childish laughter had once echoed in this room, though nothing of him remained there. I frowned; I still didn't have the whole picture, and Dr. Marsh had rattled me.

I opened all the cupboards. The remnants of Eric's babyhood—plastic formula bottles and Barney sippy cups—had been stowed on the higher shelves.

No Nestle's Quik.

"Any conclusions?" Richard asked.

"Whatever I'm getting seems strongest in the kitchen." I leaned against the counter, stared at the refrigerator covered with torn-out coloring book pages attached with yellowing Scotch tape. Something about it bothered me. I opened the door.

Paula wasn't taking care of herself. A quart of outdated skim milk, half a loaf of sliced white bread, a sagging pizza box and three two-liter bottles of diet cola looked lonely in the full-sized fridge. No chocolate milk. An opened box of Tater Tots, a sprinkling of damp crumbs, and a couple of ice trays were the only things in the freezer. Everything looked completely innocent, yet something was terribly wrong.

"Think all the apartments are set up the same?" I asked Richard.

He shrugged.

Pushing away from the counter, I walked through the rooms one last time—just to make certain—then paused in the kitchen before heading into the building's entryway. No trace of Eric, but something else lurked there.

Hands thrust into her jacket pockets, Paula waited by the security door, looking pale and frightened. I couldn't even muster a comforting smile for her.

"Chocolate milk," I said.

She blinked.

"Did Eric drink it?" I pressed.

"He loved it, but was allergic to chocolate. I never had it in the house."

I glanced up the shadowy staircase. A wounded animal will always climb. Eric hadn't been wounded, but something had lured him up those stairs. I took three steps and staggered against the banister when a knife-thrust of pain pierced the back of my head—fierce, but unlike the skull-pounding headaches these intuitive flashes usually brought.

"You okay?" Richard asked, concerned. Was he feeling guilty for roping me into this?

I leaned against the wall, closed my eyes and tried to catch my breath. "Who lives upstairs?" I asked Paula through gritted teeth.

"Mark and Cheryl Spencer in apartment D. A retired widow, Mrs. Anna Jarowski, lives on the other side."

"They see Eric the day he disappeared?"

Paula shook her head. "No."

I took another step. The heaviness clamped tighter around my chest. I'd felt something when I first entered the building, but I'd assumed it belonged to Paula.

I'd been wrong.

"I want to talk to them."

"They've been cleared," Paula insisted.

I didn't budge.

She bristled with impatience. "You came here to find answers about my son, not waste time questioning my neighbors. They've been cleared by the police, and badgered by the press."

"Paula," Richard said gently. "It can't hurt."

Finally she tore her gaze from mine and stormed back for her apartment, letting the door bang shut.

Richard took the lead, leaving Dr. Marsh and me to

follow. He went to knock on the first apartment door, but I shook my head. He gave me a quizzical look and I nodded toward the opposite door.

Richard crossed the ten or so feet to the adjacent door and knocked. We waited. Were Richard and Dr. Marsh struck by the unnatural quiet in that building?

The door opened on a chain. Steel gray, no-nonsense eyes peered at us. "Yes?"

"Mrs. Jarowski, I'm Doctor Alpert and this is Dr. Marsh," Richard said with authority. "We're from the University. May we speak with you?"

Mrs. Jarowski blinked in surprise. "Did Dr. Adams send you?"

Dr. Marsh gave Richard an inquisitive look, but he said nothing.

Mrs. Jarowski looked at us with suspicion. "Can I see some identification?"

"Of course," Richard said, and reached into his coat pocket.

"I left mine in my purse," Dr. Marsh said.

Mrs. Jarowski scrutinized Richard's hospital security badge. "Please come in," she said at last.

I didn't want to. I wanted to go home. I wanted to be anywhere but this place that smelled of mothballs and sour cabbage.

She ushered us inside, stepping into her kitchen. Anna Jarowski was a compact woman in her mid-sixties. Her short silver hair was caught back from her forehead with a barrette, like something out of the 1950s. Dressed in a faded housecoat, no make-up brightened her wan features, leaving her looking colorless and ill.

She glanced at me. "I'm sorry, but I didn't catch your name."

"Jeffrey Resnick," I said, forcing a smile, and shoved my hand at her.

The woman eyed my outstretched hand, hesitated,

then took it.

Our eyes locked. Her hand convulsed around mine. Peering past the layers of her personality, I looked straight into her soul.

A tremor ran through me. I pulled back my hand, my legs suddenly rubbery. Sweat soaked into my shirt collar and I took a shaky breath, hoping to quell the queasiness in my gut.

"Mind if I sit?"

She gestured toward the couch in the living room, but I lurched into the kitchen and fell into a maple chair at the worn Formica table. The others followed, leaning against the counters, looking like wallflowers at a dance. Mrs. Jarowski moved to stand in front of the refrigerator, arms at her side, body tense. The open floor plan allowed me to look into the apartment. Like the kitchen set, the rest of the furniture was shabby but immaculate. Mrs. Jarowski's faded house dress was freshly ironed. She probably spent her days scrubbing the life out of things.

I looked around the sterile kitchen, an exact replica of the room directly below us—the floor, the counters, the cupboards—everything, right down to the white plastic switch plates. Three embroidered dishtowels lined the oven door pull, Mrs. Jarowski's only concession to decor. The tug of conflicting emotions was even stronger than downstairs. We looked at one another for a few moments in awkward silence.

Mrs. Jarowski cleared her throat. "Are you a doctor, too?" she asked me.

"You might say I'm an expert on headaches. Tell me about yours, Mrs. Jarowski. Migraines, aren't they?"

The old lady's sharp eyes softened. "I've had a lot of tests, even a couple of CAT scans, but they've all been inconclusive. I've been told they're due to stress. One doctor said they're psychosomatic."

"I doubt that," I said, winning a grateful nod. "They

get pretty bad sometimes, don't they?"

She nodded again, looking hopeful.

"I can sure identify with that. I got mugged last year. A teenager with a baseball bat cracked my skull. Since then I get some really bad ones. I'm working up to a doozie right now."

"What does that have to do with me?" she asked, an odd catch to her voice.

"Nothing. Tell me about Eric Devlin."

Her back went rigid. "I've already told the police, I don't know anything about his disappearance."

"His mother said he was 'all boy,' but I get the feeling he was a little hellion. A noisy kid. Kind of a brat, really."

Dr. Marsh glared at me as if I'd blasphemed God Almighty. The whole city had developed a reverence for the missing child.

Mrs. Jarowski didn't share that feeling.

"He used to ride up and down the sidewalk on one of those big plastic tricycles for hours at a time. Up and down and up and down. They make one hell of a racket, don't they?"

Her lips tightened. The tension in that kitchen nearly crackled.

My nausea cranked up a notch and I loosened my tie. On the verge of passing out, I rested my elbows on the table to steady myself.

"When I have one of these sick headaches, I have to lie down in a dark room with absolute quiet. Otherwise I think I'd go insane. That ever happen to you?"

Mrs. Jarowski's gaze pinned me.

The vision streaked before my mind's eye: Eric, eyes round with anticipation, his small hand clutching the tumbler of chocolate milk, something his mother would never let him have. Paula calling to him from somewhere outside. The half empty glass falling to the spotless floor, shattering. Chocolate milk splashing the walls and cabinet doors.

"It's peaceful and quiet these days," I said. "Like a morgue." My gaze drifted to the full-sized refrigerator—back to her. I swallowed down bile. "You want to show me?"

Her cheeks flushed. She wouldn't look at me.

Dr. Marsh and Richard looked at me in confusion. Mrs. Jarowski seemed to weigh the question, her solemn gaze focused on the floor.

"The freezer, right?"

Mrs. Jarowski's anger slipped, replaced by a tremendous sense of guilt—but not, I noticed, remorse.

"Dr. Alpert, maybe you should have a look."

She held her ground.

Richard brushed past me, crossed the room in three steps. His eyes bored into hers and she backed down, moving aside. The freezer door swung open. A heavy, black plastic garbage bag filled the space. He worked on the twist tie, pulled back the plastic. His breath caught and he slammed the door, suddenly pale.

"Holy Christ."

The quartz wall clock ticked loudly, but time seemed to stand still.

At last Richard moved to the phone and punched 911. "I'm calling to report a body at 456 Weatherby, apartment C."

Richard swallowed as he listened to the voice on the other end of the phone. Dr. Marsh blinked in confused revulsion.

Stony-faced, Mrs. Jarowski turned, her slippered feet scuffing across the vinyl floor as she headed for the living room. She sat down on her faded couch, picked up the remote control and turned on the television.

Finally Richard hung up the phone.

"Dr. Marsh, can you watch Mrs. J until the police get here?" I asked.

She nodded, still looking shell shocked.

I squinted up at Richard. "Maybe you could help me to the bathroom. I don't want to barf on Mrs. J's nice clean floor."

Breathing shallowly, I sat back against the lumpy couch, a hand covering my eyes to blot out the piercing light. After more than an hour, two of my pills still hadn't put a dent in the throbbing headache.

The cops had already taken Mrs. Jarowski away. The ME arrived, and the crime photographer was still flashing pictures in the kitchen. The place was full of cops, and the murmur of a dozen voices drilled through my skull.

"Can I get you something, Mr. Resnick?" Lieutenant Brewer of the Buffalo Metropolitan Police stood over me. The chunky, balding cop still seemed taken aback that his case had been broken by an outsider.

I squinted up at him. "Yeah. Assure my privacy— don't give the press my name. The last thing I want is publicity."

"Okay, but answer me this: how'd you know?"

"I don't know how it works, it just does."

"The old lady waived her rights. Said she heard Ms. Devlin had signed a new two-year lease and decided she'd had enough of the noise. She lured the kid up here and made him quiet—permanently."

"And the chocolate milk?" Richard asked me.

"The lure of a forbidden treat. Mrs. J ground up sleeping pills, had him drink it," I said. "When he was dopey, she planned to smother him."

I thought about it—remembered what I'd seen when I'd touched her. Fury gave her the strength to hold the boy, who'd struggled in those last minutes. She'd sealed his nose and mouth with a wad of freshly pressed linen dish towels, pinning him against the floor until his body slackened, his small chest no longer heaving. Then she'd heard Paula Devlin frantically calling for her son. Anna Jarowski sat beside the dead boy for a long time—triumphant in the knowledge she'd finally silenced her intolerably noisy neighbor.

I looked up at Brewer. "I take it you haven't searched the place yet."

"Call me paranoid, but I'm waiting for a warrant. No way do I want this thrown out on a technicality."

"You'll find what's left of the tricycle in one of the closets. She's got a hacksaw. Been cutting it up and sneaking it out in the trash for the past eight months."

Dr. Marsh elbowed her way through the crowd in the kitchen. She'd been gone about an hour—breaking the news to the boy's mother, no doubt.

"How's Paula?" Richard asked.

"I gave her a sedative. Now that her mother's here, I think she'll be all right." She looked at me. "How are you, Jeff?" Her icy veneer had melted, her best bedside manner now firmly in place.

"Sick."

"But you've got to feel good about what you've done."

I frowned. "I made two women miserable. Why would that make me feel good?"

She seemed puzzled by my answer, but I didn't have the energy to explain it to her. "Dr. Marsh, you said another psychic came here—what did she tell Paula?"

"That the boy was well and living in a small town down South, anxious to be back home with his mother."

Poor Paula.

"You need me anymore?" I asked the detective.

He shook his head. "Go home before you keel over."

I glanced at my brother. "Now would be a good time, Rich."

I moved on shaky legs. Richard and Dr. Marsh steadied me on the stairs. We ducked under the crime scene tape and they pushed me through the throng of press as we headed for Richard's Lincoln Town Car.

Dr. Marsh crushed her business card into my palm. "Call me." Her voice was husky, excited, like a rock star's groupie.

Reporters and cameramen swarmed as she slammed the car door. Richard left her to deal with them, taking off with a squeal and leaving rubber on the asphalt.

"Sharks," he muttered.

I leaned against the headrest and considered my first consultation. By all counts, a royal success.

Then why did I feel so dirty?

The trick-or-treaters have gone home and now it's time for the adults to celebrate All Hallows Eve. When Maggie suggests they consult a Ouija board, Jeff Resnick thinks it'll be anything but fun. And when they conjure up a ghost from Jeff's past, the game turns dangerous for the most vulnerable person in his life.

SPOOKED

I flipped the switch and the brass lamps outside the big oak front door winked out. The candy was all gone. Halloween was over—at least for the neighborhood kids. It was time for the adults to kick back and have their turn.

Mind you, I'd grown up in a part of Buffalo where kids didn't go out at night—even with an adult escort—and I wasn't one of the lucky ones who'd been loaded into the back of a van and driven to the 'burbs to enjoy that childhood pleasure, either. So except for parties at school, where I never dressed up in costume—there wasn't any money for that trifle—Halloween had never really been on my holiday radar. Maggie and Brenda, however, seized any opportunity to celebrate.

The pumpkins, gourds, and other orange-and-yellow decorations had started showing up the second week of October. Brenda had decided to dress up as a witch—"a good witch," she clarified—her flowing skirt and cape camouflaging the weight she hadn't yet lost since giving birth three weeks before to my niece, the most beautiful baby in the world: Betsy Ruth Alpert. No brag; just fact. Before being settled in her bassinette an hour before, Betsy had been dressed in her first Halloween costume as Hello Kitty and I had taken at least two dozen photos of her. We'd already printed enough to fill two albums, and had hours of video chronicling her gassy smiles, pouts, squirms, cries, and snippets of her sleeping in heavenly peace.

I bypassed the living room, turning out more lights as I went, and headed for my brother Richard's study. That's where my girlfriend Maggie, Richard, and Brenda, had camped for the evening. I found them parked around the coffee table, where Brenda was doling out slices of pizza on paper plates, accompanied by black napkins decorated with a jumble of snaggle-toothed orange pumpkins.

"Did you get onions?" I asked, plopping down beside Maggie on the long leather couch. She looked cute dressed in a short black dress, black fishnet stockings, boots, and a tall pointed black witch's hat. Later I hoped she might exchange the hat for a short white apron, turning her into a French maid.

"Onions, peppers, mushrooms, sausage, and pepperoni," Richard recited. "Isn't that what you requested?"

"Suggested," I corrected him, taking possession of a slice goopy with what looked like a double helping of mozzarella cheese. "Thank you, Brenda."

Maggie handed me a sweating bottle of Labatt Blue. She was drinking her favorite whisky sour. Richard had single malt scotch on the rocks, and Brenda was savoring a glass of Pinot Grigio. She'd gone without wine for the better part of a year during her first pregnancy, which had ended in miscarriage, and then again this year. "How many kids did we have?" Richard asked, accepting a wedge of pizza.

"Forty-seven," Maggie reported, and took a bite of her own goopy slice. "Mmm."

It was good pizza, with a nice chewy crust, and nothing tasted better with a cold beer.

"What was the most popular costume?" Richard asked.

"Zombies, followed by ghosts, pirates, and princesses," Maggie said. She'd pulled candy-distribution duty while Brenda saw to the baby and Richard and I had hunkered down here in the study, playing chess and making do with chips and dip until the pizza arrived.

"Maybe next year we should throw a Halloween party," Maggie said.

"I haven't been to a Halloween party since I was in college," Richard said.

"I haven't been to one since sixth grade," I said.

"When I was a girl, we always bobbed for apples," Brenda said. "It was my sister Ruthie's favorite thing, but not mine. I didn't like getting my face all wet."

"Me, either," Maggie agreed. "Besides, I preferred candy to apples."

"Me, too," Brenda said.

"Apples should be reserved for pies," I said, giving Maggie a hopeful look. Nobody makes a better apple pie than she does.

She ignored the hint. "Low-key parties can be just as enjoyable as big boisterous ones. After we finish the pizza, we can play a few games."

"Games? You mean like charades?" I asked with dread.

"Yeah, we could play that, too."

"I like charades, but I can't imagine Jeffy would," Brenda said, eyeing me, and grinned. "What else did you have in mind?"

Maggie set down her pizza slice and reached for the canvas bag that was stationed by her left knee. From it, she pulled a long slender rectangular box. I had a feeling I knew what it would be even before I saw the picture on the top.

I wasn't wrong.

"A Ouija board?" Brenda asked. Richard and I groaned, but Brenda seemed keen to play. "I haven't done this since I was a kid back in Philly," she practically squealed. "Ruthie and I weren't allowed to mess with the occult, as my mother called it, so we had to play the game on overnights at our friend Nancy's house. We scared each other half to death on more than one occasion."

"I'm with your mother," Richard said. "Messing with the occult could be dangerous."

"Oh, you don't really believe in all that, do you?" Maggie asked. "It's only a game."

Richard looked over at me. "I might have agreed a few years ago, but since Jeff came back to Buffalo, I'm no longer a skeptic."

All three of them looked at me, and suddenly I felt like a leper. I shrugged. "There was a presence in this house when I first came back—it scared the shit out of me. I'm not sure I want to invite it back."

"Oh, for heaven's sake—there are no such things as ghosts," Maggie cried.

Richard and I shared a knowing glance.

"It'll be fun." Maggie said with what sounded like glee. Sometimes I wondered what such a happy soul ever saw in me.

Fun? We had distinctly different ideas about that word. Maggie was the type who loved a roller coaster ride, enjoyed splashing around in a pool, and would love to dance until her legs fell off. Me? Not so much.

She moved the plate full of ghost and pumpkin cutout cookies she'd made and decorated for the occasion, as well as the pizza box to one side and set up the board.

"I've never played with one of these things. What do we do?" Richard asked, apparently resigned to the idea of playing the so-called game.

Maggie set the white plastic heart-shaped pointer in the middle of the Ouija board. "We all place a finger on the planchette, then we ask the board a question. If the spirits are active, and they should be tonight of all nights, they'll spell out an answer."

"How do we know if one of us cheats?" Richard asked.

"I trust all of you with my life," Maggie said sincerely. "I have faith you'll all be honest in whatever game we played."

Ha! She'd never played Richard at one-on-one basketball.

"I'd like to finish my pizza first," I said.

"Me, too," Brenda agreed. "And I want to check on the baby."

Maggie picked up her slice. "Fine with me."

The CD player clanked as it changed disks, and one of Beethoven's more brooding sonatas began. Richard is a classical music freak. I prefer light jazz, and Maggie listens to soft rock, while Brenda enjoys disco. When in Richard's domain, we listened to his musical preferences.

We each finished another slice of pizza before Brenda went upstairs to check on Princess Betsy. We heard her whisper "sweet dreams" from the baby monitor that sat on the side table next to Brenda's end of the long leather couch. A minute later, she rejoined us.

The ladies cleared away the pizza box, soiled plates and napkins, and then Maggie roamed around the room, lowering the lights. Finally she was ready to start the game.

"I don't know about this," I said when Maggie resumed her seat beside me. "Aren't you afraid of conjuring up an evil spirit?"

Maggie laughed. "Don't worry. I read somewhere that our subconscious minds are the ones that actually move the planchette."

"Telekinesis isn't one of my gifts," I said sincerely. Since I'd been bonked on the head with a baseball bat some nineteen months before during a mugging that had very nearly killed me, I'd become aware of things that others weren't aware of. I knew things others didn't know—saw things others couldn't see. Some people called it a gift. Some called me psychic. I called myself damned unlucky.

Maggie laughed again. "Oh, Jeff, don't look so serious. It's just a game."

Maybe it was to her, but I could see by Richard's concerned expression that it was no game to him, either. And yet, neither of us made another objection.

Stupid.

"What are you going to ask first?" Brenda asked, her right index finger hovering over the planchette, ready to begin.

"What else?" Maggie set her finger on the planchette and the rest of us did likewise. "Is there anybody out there?"

The planchette immediately started to move. It scraped around the board, making lazy circles around the letters before it stopped at the first one.

Y.

It circled again.

E.

And again.

S.

It stopped.

Maggie smiled, delighted. "Yes! Well, of course."

"Why didn't the spirit just point the planchette to the word yes on the board?" I asked.

"Showing off?" Richard guessed.

Maggie gave us each a frown, then addressed the board again. "Are you friendly?"

The pointer began to circle the board once again before it slid toward the word NO, but then it did an abrupt about face and landed on YES.

"Whew!" Maggie said. "For a moment there, I thought we might be in trouble."

Richard caught my eye. He wasn't smiling. The pizza in my stomach seemed to be trying out some salsa moves and I wished I hadn't had that second slice.

"I have a question," Richard said in all seriousness.

"Ask away," Maggie said.

He stared at the board intently. "Will the Bills ever win the Super Bowl?"

"When hell freezes over," Brenda said.

"Not funny," Richard deadpanned, eyeing her coldly.

We all turned our attention back to the board when the planchette began moving around once again. For a moment, it seemed to be veering toward YES, but then suddenly slid completely off the board.

"Well, it didn't say no," Maggie said. She was ever hopeful. "Any other questions?"

I shook my head, saying nothing.

Maggie sighed. "I guess I should have come up with a few more, but honestly, I thought you guys would be more in the spirit of things. It is, after all, Halloween."

"I'm game," Richard said. He looked back down at the board. "Tell us what's beyond this life."

"Do you really want to know?" Brenda asked, aghast.

"I'm Catholic. I already know," Richard said.

I wasn't sure I wanted to know, either. I had some ideas, and I didn't need them verified. I felt much better not knowing for sure.

The planchette began its journey around the board once again. Maggie called out the letters as it paused. "S-T-A-R-L-I-G-H-T. Starlight? What does that mean?"

Richard shrugged. "The heavens are full of stars."

"What a nice thought," Maggie said, smiling. "Do you have another message for us?" she asked the board.

The planchette jerked beneath our fingers and madly began to race around the board—once, twice, three times before it stopped on the letter G. Maggie began to read out the letters as it stopped and started in what seemed like a haphazard fashion.

E-T-O-U-T-O-F-M-Y-H-O-U-S-E.

Maggie frowned. "Get out of my house? Well, that wasn't very nice." She addressed the board once again. "Who?"

The planchette stopped moving as abruptly as it had begun, then went skidding in Brenda's direction, startling her—but then it circled round the board again before it practically flew at me.

"Whoa! That's some serious specter," Maggie quipped, and picked up the indicator. She set it back on the board. "Come on, everyone; put your fingers back on it."

"I don't want to play," Richard said.

"Don't you want to know who the message is directed at?"

"I have a pretty good idea already," Brenda said, no longer enthused to play the game.

"Come on," Maggie encouraged.

The three of us looked at one another, but then let Maggie bully us into participating once again.

"Who do you want out of the house?" Maggie asked.

The planchette moved around the board once again, landing on the letter B.

Brenda winced.

Next, it traveled to the letter L.

Richard watched in horror as the next letters A-C-K.

"Wow," Maggie murmured, "a racist ghost."

I had a pretty good idea who that ghost might have been, too, and stared at the indicator as it spelled out yet another two words: A-N-D-T-R-A-S-H, then halted so that the front of the planchette pointed directly at me.

"I think we've both just been insulted," I said, but didn't laugh.

Brenda pulled back her hand. "I am not going to be slurred by a game."

I folded my arms across my chest. "Me, either."

Maggie frowned. "This has never happened when I've played the game before."

Maybe because this was no longer a game.

Suddenly the bulb in the lamp next to me exploded in a flash of blue light, scaring the hell out of all of us. Both Maggie and Brenda let out yelps of surprise, which gave both Richard and me another start.

"Holy crap," I managed. "Don't do that!"

"Well, it scared me," Maggie said, defending herself.

"I'll go get another bulb," Richard volunteered, when the lamp on his desk suddenly blew, too. "What the hell?"

"Maybe it's some kind of electrical surge," Brenda offered as an explanation.

I turned my head in the direction of Richard's desk, which was now shrouded in darkness. The entire room seemed to shimmer around me, and when my vision cleared, Richard, Brenda, and Maggie seemed to have gone into suspended animation—not so for the other presence that had joined us.

I recognized the old lady. How could I ever forget the woman who had driven my mother insane? Who had stolen her child. Who had made my own life hell on a daily basis for almost four years. Margery Alpert: Richard's long-dead grandmother.

I rose to my feet. "What the hell are you doing here?"

"What are *you* doing in *my* house?" the apparition before me demanded in her cold voice. Cold as the grave, where she belonged.

"I thought we got rid of you more than a year ago."

"I did, too, but someone called me back, and this time I don't intend to leave, at least not as long as *you're* here. And who is *that*?" she demanded, pointing at Brenda.

I debated answering. The old bat had hated me. While she'd employed an elderly black man as her chauffeur for many years, I wasn't certain she had ever liked Curtis

Johnson. I had loved the old man, who'd taken me under his wing and shown me infinite kindness when no one else in that house could be bothered to do so. How would she react to find out Brenda was Richard's wife?

I didn't have a chance to speak. Her gaze traveled around the room and settled on the framed picture that sat on one of the bookshelves across the way.

The old woman's eyes widened in disbelief and suddenly she jerked forward, her cane thumping on the parquet floor, her rubber-soled shoes squeaking as she pivoted to round the empty wing chair to her right. She stomped across the floor and stared at the photo. I could feel her anger rise to a near boil as her parchment-like skin began to redden as though sunburned.

Brenda's smile had been beatific on that sunny day in June the year before. Her ivory tea-length dress had been understated, yet lovely. Richard's shiner, the remnant of an unfortunate encounter with a bigot, had begun to fade but was still evident in all their wedding photos. "Photoshop is my best friend," Richard had assured Brenda, but she'd shaken her head, saying she'd prefer he leave them as they were so they'd have a good story to tell their children one day. So far, he hadn't entertained baby Betsy with that bedtime tale.

Mrs. Alpert turned to glare at her grandson. "How could he do this to me?" she accused. "How?" she demanded, loud enough to wake the dead.

Instead, it was an infant's cry that issued from the baby monitor on the end table. What the hell? The rest of them seemed to be frozen in a moment of time. Did that unearthly spell only apply to that room—to those people?

"What was that?" Mrs. Alpert demanded.

"What was what?" I answered stupidly.

The baby cried once again. It was her fretful cry—perhaps a wet diaper. In three short weeks I could read her pretty well. Sometimes she wouldn't sleep for her Mom and Pop. I'd see the lights on late at night when I came in from my stint behind the bar at The Whole Nine Yards and drop in, giving them a break from walking the floor. That little girl and I already had a rapport. I'd rock her in the chair beside her bassinette and she'd fall asleep in no time flat. She was my little cherry pie, and no uncle could have been more proud.

But it wasn't pride I felt just then. It was terror. The same terror I'd felt when I'd first returned to that house after an eighteen-year absence. I knew what the old lady was capable of. She'd killed before.

Old lady Alpert turned on her heel, her cane thumping against the floor once again as she headed for the hall and the stairs to the second floor.

"Oh, no you don't," I shouted, and ran after her, but when I got to the hall, she'd vanished.

I went after her, but it seemed like my legs were slogging through mud. By the time I made it to the foot of the stairs, I could hear clomping footsteps from up above, heading toward what used to be my bedroom—what was now the nursery.

Panic lent me speed as I rounded the corner and raced up the stairs two at a time, but I wasn't able to catch up with whatever was left of that hateful woman.

The door to the baby's room was open, but it seemed like the hall stretched a million miles ahead as I moved at an agonizingly slow pace. When I finally rounded the doorway, I found the old woman in the darkened room standing over the baby's bassinette. Betsy was awake, watching the mobile of pastel bugs bobbing and weaving over her head.

I flipped the switch, but it seemed an eternity until the light came on. Unfortunately, the apparition did not disappear in the stark, bright light. "Get away from her," I said, but my voice came out a long, slow growl.

I leapt forward, intending to knock her down, just as time seemed to resume its normal speed. But I sailed through empty air, landing painfully hard on my stomach. For a moment, I thought my pizza dinner might make a reappearance. When I looked up again, the old woman was standing on the other side of the bassinette. "Get away from her," I said again.

"Is she Richard's?" she demanded.

"Of course she is."

"What's her name?" she demanded.

"Betsy Ruth."

"Betsy? Don't you mean Elizabeth—like that whoring bitch?"

"That's my mother you're referring to," I warned. "You didn't think he'd name his first-born after you, did you?"

"Why wouldn't he?"

"Because he didn't love you."

Her eyes widened, her cheeks flushing. "That's a lie."

"Guess how many people were at your funeral?"

The idea that she might actually be dead seemed to jack up her anger but she said nothing.

"Two. A priest and Curtis Johnson. You didn't deserve even that," I said angrily, "not the way you treated Curtis, and not with the mortal sin that will forever blacken your soul."

Her glare was baleful, but she didn't deny it.

Betsy gurgled, kicking her feet in the air, drawing the old lady's attention away from me. "Mulatto," she growled.

"That's a vulgar term. She's mixed race," I corrected her through clenched teeth. If she wasn't already dead, I would have liked to have slugged her. "Why don't you just go to hell where you belong?"

"This is *my* house."

"Not anymore. And there's nothing for you here. No

love, and for damn sure, no forgiveness."

"I don't need *your* forgiveness."

"And you sure as hell won't get Richard's either. Now, why don't you just go back to whatever purgatory you've been sentenced to and never bother us again?"

"This is my house," she repeated.

Were we going to be stuck with this Halloween witch for the rest of our lives? There had to be a way to get rid of her once and for all, but for the life of me I couldn't think of anything short of exorcism. Her malevolent spirit had been banished when I'd discovered the terrible crime she'd committed. Would reminding her of it cause her to leave once again? And what if it didn't? Would she hang around annoying Brenda, or worse—could she hurt Betsy?

I wasn't about to let that happen.

Mrs. Alpert was still staring at her great granddaughter, her lip curled in contempt.

"There's part of you in that little girl," I said, lamenting the fact.

My words seemed to have struck a nerve with her. Her head jerked up, her eyes wide. She stared at me for a long moment and then looked back at the baby. Her eyes filled with tears and she quickly looked away.

"She's your great granddaughter—your flesh and blood," I pressed, hoping that might inspire some molecule of family pride, but instead my words seemed to agitate her. The old woman shook her head and began to cry in earnest. "She'll carry your genes into the next generation," I said, and she shook her head even harder.

"Stop it—stop tormenting me," she cried.

I wasn't sure what to say next, so I stood there waiting and watching.

Mrs. Alpert wiped her eyes and seemed to get her emotions under control. She stared at little Betsy, who was still merrily kicking away. The old lady reached for the baby, but I caught her wrist, which turned out to be solid in my grasp.

"Don't touch her," I grated, as protective as a mother bear.

"I wasn't going to hurt her," Mrs. Alpert said, then frowned. "She is a pretty little thing, but she isn't mine."

"Why do you say that?"

She shook her head, still staring at Betsy. "Because … because John wasn't my son."

I blinked in surprise. "Whose son was he?"

The old woman looked up to glare at me. "My husband's *love* child."

Old Mr. Alpert had stepped out on the old lady? No wonder she'd made his life a living hell. "But how did you end up with him?"

"I couldn't have children. We paid her a lot of money to leave the state and never contact us again."

"So, not only did you take John away from his mother, you did the same to Richard, too," I said with disgust.

She said nothing, didn't look ashamed, and why had I expected more from her? She'd been an evil witch in life, and death hadn't changed her.

I let go of her wrist.

Her gaze moved from the baby to take in the rest of the room, which looked nothing like it had when it was mine. Finally, she looked at me once again. "I never liked you."

"The feeling was mutual."

She nodded, and it seemed like all the fight had left her, leaving her looking old and worn out—no doubt, as she'd looked when she'd breathed her last breath. "I suppose you're right after all. This isn't my house anymore."

"No, it isn't. It hasn't been for a long time."

She looked back down at Betsy, who'd closed her eyes and was sleeping once again. "Have a happy life, little girl. May it be far happier than mine ever was."

And whose fault was that?

As I looked at her, the old woman seemed to dissolve in front of me, the image of her growing more and more transparent until she'd completely disappeared.

So, the old girl had had one last secret to reveal, one last confession to make. Now that that burden had been lifted from her soul, would she finally enter eternal rest or was she facing the fires of damnation? I couldn't work up much interest either way—I just hoped she was gone for good.

I took one long last look at my little Cherry Pie, then turned, switched off the light, and left the door open.

The house was eerily quiet as I made my way down the stairs. When I got back to Richard's study, I nearly ran into him as he came out of the darkened room.

"You were right behind me. How did you get out in the hall before me?"

"You wouldn't believe me if I told you." I thought better of it. "Then again, maybe you might. Get the new light bulbs, pour me a drink, and I'll share one hell of a Halloween story with you."

HAVE DIAPER BAG—WILL TRAVEL!

Jeff Resnick—babysitter? It wasn't a reference that had ever graced his personal résumé, but when he's entrusted to care for his brother's most prized possession—his infant daughter—Jeff is tested in ways he could never have anticipated. With his girlfriend Maggie unavailable, Jeff has only one person he can turn to for advice when his tiny niece falls ill on his watch.

CRYBABY

"You've got our cell phone numbers," my older, half-brother Richard Alpert said, his gaze deadly serious. "They'll work until we get to the border. After that, we'll be out of communication until we get to the hotel. I left that number, plus the restaurant and theater's, as well as a list of other emergency numbers on the fridge. And, of course, if worse comes to worst, you can always call 911."

I let out a long—a very L-O-N-G—breath and nodded. How many times had he lectured me in the past few weeks about the same thing? Richard and his wife, Brenda, were heading for an overnight in Toronto. As a Christmas gift to her, he'd bought tickets to see the Canadian version of the hottest play on Broadway and my lady, Maggie Brennan, and I were going to be entrusted with Richard's and Brenda's most prized possession—if you wanted to objectify her in that way—their four-month-old daughter, Elizabeth Ruth.

They called her Betsy, after Richard's and my mother, but to me she was CP, otherwise known as Cherry Pie. Why? Because before she was even conceived, I knew that little girl was destined to be born and had bought her several little red dresses (in various sizes) decorated with white polka-dots and miniature cherries. You see, almost two years before, I'd been viciously mugged and suffered a serious brain injury. As a consequence, I'm just a little bit psychic. Not that I'd say the 'p' word out loud to anyone. To be perfectly correct, I'm empathic—sort of like Counselor Troi from Star Trek. Only, most of the time, my ability is more hit-and-miss, and sometimes I just know things that I could not know by any other means.

"It's not like I don't know how to take care of a baby," I told my big brother—the ever-worried physician. Since CP had arrived, I'd spent my fair share of time taking care of that precious little girl. Not only had I changed wet and stinky diapers, but that tiny girl and I had bonded in a very special way, thanks to said head injury.

I worked nights at a local bar called The Whole Nine Yards and often came home after two in the morning. I live in the apartment over the garage on Richard's property. If I arrive home in the wee hours and see the lights on at the big house, I know CP is having a bad night. That also means her parents are having a bad night. Since I need time to wind down after hours of pouring drinks for thirsty Buffalonians, I use my key to enter the house to relieve a grateful mom and pop from walking the floor.

I rarely worked the more lucrative weekend shifts, so Maggie and I were more than happy to give Richard and Brenda (who also happens to be Maggie's best friend), a short respite from parenthood. That is, if they would ever leave.

"If we hit the road by ten tomorrow morning, we could be back in time for lunch," Richard said.

"Wait a minute," Brenda interrupted. "You mean I don't get time to shop?"

"I thought you wanted to stop for afternoon tea in Niagara-On-The-Lake on the way home," I said.

"That, too," Brenda eagerly agreed.

Richard seemed to squirm in his heavy winter coat. "I don't want to abuse your generosity. This is a *big* responsibility," he told me gravely.

Yes, it was. But Maggie and I were more than quali-fied to take on the task.

"Go. Enjoy yourselves. And don't worry. You'll be gone a little over twenty-four hours. What could possi-bly happen in that short amount of time?"

Richard opened his mouth as though to give me an extended list of possible disasters, but Brenda leapt for-ward and clamped a hand over his lips. "Don't you dare even speculate," she admonished him.

"You know I'd give my life for CP, but I really don't think that's going to be necessary. At least not tonight."

"Me, either," Brenda said.

"When's Maggie going to get here?" Richard asked.

Hey! I was the one who'd changed diapers and walked the floor with CP on many a cold winter's night. Maggie had a niece and several nephews, but hadn't had all that much experience with infants. Why did Richard seem to think that her two X chromosomes were more valuable when it came to childcare?

"Don't worry. Maggie will be here after she gets off work—about five thirty. I'm sure CP and I can manage for the next few hours without her," I assured him.

His expression was still grave. "Okay," he said at last. He consulted his watch. "I guess we'd better get going. I'll just go up and give Betsy a good-night kiss...."

"Oh, no you won't," Brenda said. "She's asleep. I don't want you waking her. Now let's go—now!"

Richard still looked skeptical.

"Rich, I know you trust me with *your* life. Can you give me the benefit of the doubt that I'll look after CP, too?"

As Richard had once—literally—taken a bullet for me, he had to know I'd do the same for him—*and* CP. "Yes," he admitted. "I know you will." He looked in Brenda's di-rection. "Okay. Let's go."

"About time, too," she muttered, then turned to me

and leaned up to give my cheek a kiss. "Take care of my girl, Jeffy."

"I will," I promised.

"We'll see you tomorrow," Richard said.

"I'll be here." I followed them to the back door and watched them cross the driveway to the garage side door. A minute later, Richard backed out his Mercedes, turning so that the front of the car faced the road. They waved and the garage door went back down as they took off down the driveway. Snowflakes slowly drifted down. I hoped they wouldn't hit any nasty weather on the two-hour drive.

I closed the back door and suddenly noticed how quiet the house was. I'd lived there for more than three years when I'd been a teenager—after the death of Richard's and my mother—but it had never felt like any kind of a home to me during the years when Richard's paternal grandparents had been alive. The old lady had been a shrew and the old man was pussy-whipped by his antagonistic wife. The vibes were different since Richard and Brenda had taken over the manse. It wasn't—and never would be—my home, but it did feel homier. CP would enjoy growing up here, something her dad could never claim.

I settled at the kitchen table with that morning's *Buffalo News* and thought about brewing a fresh pot of coffee, but then decided against it. CP had been sleeping through the night for the past couple of weeks and I hoped that Maggie and I would be able to do the same. Maggie and I would never have kids of our own, but we had no problem spoiling CP—not that you could do all that much for so young a child.

I read the newspaper, but half of my attention was tuned to the baby monitor that sat on the kitchen counter. If CP woke, I'd hear her cries.

It made me smile when I thought of how much that

baby had changed all our lives. Her presence had been a bridge for Brenda to reconnect with her estranged family. CP had given me, Richard, Brenda, and even Maggie, the best Christmas any of us had had in years. Maggie surprised us all—even tiny CP—with ugly Christmas sweaters. Thanks to the timer on my digital camera, we had a fantastic geeky shot of the five of us that we could haul out and laugh at for years to come: Maggie, me, and Brenda looking manic, while a dour Richard held up a sleepy CP, who sported a smelly diaper.

I looked at the clock on the wall. Richard and Brenda hadn't been gone more than ten minutes when I could no longer stand the silence and trundled up the stairs to check on my little niece. The door to the nursery—what had once been my bedroom—was open. I peeked inside to see CP bundled in a pink sleeper, fast asleep, just as her mommy had left her. Her breathing sounded a little noisy, but nothing to worry about. The house was dry and my nose was just a little stuffed, too.

I tiptoed from the room and went back down to the kitchen, glancing at the clock before I resumed my seat. Maggie was going to stop at the grocery store to pick up a frozen pizza for our dinner. Oh, yes, the babysitters were going to really live it up. That's what I thought. Then the phone rang. I leapt out of my chair to grab it before it could jangle once again and wake CP.

"Hello?"

"Jeff?" the voice croaked.

"Maggie?" I asked, shock and worry suddenly filling me.

"I'b sick."

"Since last night?" I asked, the muscles in my shoulders suddenly starting to bunch.

"I think I'b got the flu. I was sidding at by desk at work when I suddenly got the chills, then I started to cough. Next thing I knew, I was in the ladies room barfing my guts up."

I winced. Not an image I wanted to contemplate. "So, CP and I won't have the pleasure of your company tonight, will we?"

"There's no way I want you or Betsy to catch this. I feel like I'b going to die."

"Are you home?"

"Yes. I got in just in time to—"

"Poor, Maggs," I said to stave off a possibly more graphic description. "You ought to climb right into bed and try to get some sleep."

"I will—if I can ever stop coughing." And to prove her point, she launched into a nasty hacking fit. I held the phone away from my ear, glad I'd let Brenda talk me into getting a flu shot back in the fall.

Finally, Maggie was able to speak again. "I'b sorry to let you down. I suppose they've already left for Toronto."

"Half an hour ago."

"You could call them. I'b sure they'd turn around."

"No way. Hey, I can take care of CP for a day. I've been changing her diapers since the day she came home from the hospital. I've fed her, walked the floor with her, and I've put her down for naps, too."

"You've watched her for a couple of hours at a time—not for more than a day," Maggie pointed out.

"And have you ever taken care of your niece or nephews for an overnight?" I asked.

"Well," Maggie began, and then was overtaken by another coughing fit. "I'b got to go—literally," Maggie said, and hung up before I could tell her I hoped she'd feel better. I didn't know where to buy chicken soup that didn't come from a can, and didn't trust my admittedly shaky culinary skills to try to make it from scratch. Maybe tomorrow, once Richard and Brenda came home, I'd visit Maggie after a stop at the local Chinese takeout to buy some hot-and-sour soup.

I replaced the phone and again noticed how god-awful quiet it was in that big house. It was just CP and me now. I'd been looking forward to Maggie and me playing pseudo parents. We'd had a few hard months—okay, more than half a year—after her older sister had tried (and nearly succeeded) to break us up, but we were almost entirely back in sync and it felt good.

I looked at my watch. By now, Richard and Brenda were probably nearing the Canadian border. Once they did, their cell phones wouldn't work. They'd booked a room at one of Toronto's fanciest hotels, had reservations for dinner at a top restaurant, and then would attend the show.

I wasn't at all surprised that it was Brenda who'd craved a break—short as it was to be—from being a caregiver. She'd been taking care of Richard and me, and now CP. She deserved a one-day reprieve, and I knew she'd come home refreshed and happy. I also knew that my big brother would pretend to be happy and relaxed, but during the next twenty-four hours would fixate on worst-case scenarios. I doubted he'd enjoy the dinner, the show, or sleep a wink, and would return home tomorrow a nervous wreck. Despite Maggie's absence, I was determined to prove to him that I could handle an infant. The house would still be standing and CP and I would not only make it through the night, but we'd both be smiling. Okay, I might have to tickle that little girl for a smile, but I knew I could do it.

Richard had promised to call as soon as they got to the hotel, so I wasn't surprised when the phone rang nearly ninety minutes later.

"It's me. How's Betsy?" Richard asked.

"Hello to you, too," I said.

"Sorry, Jeff," Richard said contritely. "How's my girl?"

"Still napping."

"Are you sure?" he asked, his voice tight with worry.

"I've checked on her a couple of times. She must just

be really sleepy today."

"I hope she won't keep you and Maggie awake tonight."

I'd already decided not to admit that I'd be CP's only caretaker. I was sure Brenda trusted me with her baby girl, but not sure my brother would give me the benefit of the doubt where his daughter was concerned. He was just a little bit paranoid.

"Not to worry. I've got the magic touch to get that baby girl to sleep."

"Yes, you do," Richard admitted. "I don't know what we would have done a couple of nights if you hadn't come over and given us a break."

"If she wants to stay up late, you've got Netflix on the big-screen TV in the living room. I'm sure we can find something to watch to amuse ourselves until she gets tired again."

"Thanks."

"Glad to be of service."

"Okay, I'd better hang up so we can get to the restaurant in time for our reservation."

"Hi, Jeffy," Brenda called from somewhere in the background. "Give my baby girl a kiss from her momma and daddy."

"Tell her I will," I told Richard. "Now, go. Have a good time. And don't worry. I've got everything under control."

"You? Where's Maggie?"

"Probably in the bathroom," I said, which may or may not have been true. At that moment, he didn't have to know that she was at her own home, not his.

"Okay. We'll call you tomorrow morning."

"You don't have to. We're going to be fine."

"Yes, but I would feel better if I do."

"Okay. Whatever."

"If I haven't said thank you—"

"You just did," I reminded him. "You're stalling. Allow yourself to have a wonderful time and stop worrying," I ordered.

"I will—I will," he asserted, but I didn't for one moment believe him.

"Have fun," I commanded and we said good-bye. I hung up and heard a gurgle from the baby monitor. CP was awake. I headed out of the kitchen and up the stairs to fetch her.

By the time I reached the second floor, her gurgles had escalated to fitful cries. She probably had a wet—or worse—diaper. Sure enough, she needed a change.

I picked her up and kissed her forehead and noted that she seemed warm to the touch—warmer than normal. Her little eyes scrunched up and she started to cry in earnest.

"Oh, CP, don't cry," I told her. "I'll change you."

I put her down on the changing table and gave her a clean diaper. Her sleeper was a little damp, so I put on a clean one and then picked her up and slung her over my shoulder. Her tiny brown fingers curled into the folds of my sweatshirt and I patted her back. "It's just you and me tonight, kid. Aunt Maggie's as sick as a dog."

As though in sympathy, CP upchucked all over my shoulder. Hot sour vomit soaked through the material. The baby had barfed on me many times before, but usually I'd had a cloth diaper or a towel slung over my shoulder, and usually it happened while trying to burp her.

"CP," I wailed and set her back in her crib, where she started to howl. I pulled off the sweatshirt and tossed it into the adjoining bathroom, then I grabbed some baby wipes to clean her face. She'd messed her sleeper, too, so I rummaged in the dresser to find another. It was the last clean one. If CP staged a repeat performance, she wouldn't have anything warm to sleep in. I'd have to do a load of laundry. Brenda probably hadn't anticipated her daughter might need two clean sleepers within the space of five minutes.

"Come on, CP, calm down," I begged as big tears cascaded down her chubby cheeks. She was still crying, but it wasn't one of her usual wails. This was different; a long note of misery broken every few seconds by a hiccupping gulp.

Richard and Brenda kept the house at an even seventy-two degrees, but I was cold without my shirt. I had figured I'd bring over a change of clothes once Maggie arrived—so I had nothing to change into. While CP continued to grizzle, I ducked into Richard and Brenda's bedroom. I wasn't about to rifle through their dresser drawers, so instead I threw open the closet door and pawed through Richard's stuff until I found a flannel shirt. It wasn't an article of clothing I'd associate with him, and I'd certainly never seen him wear it, but if the baby barfed on it, it wasn't likely to get ruined, either. I donned it. Richard was almost six inches taller than me and the sleeves were miles too long, but the buttons at the cuffs at least kept them from hanging over the tips of my fingers.

I ducked back into the nursery. CP's cries had wound down to a whimper. I picked her up once more and she nestled her face against my shoulder. I wasn't sure what to do, so I sat down in the glider where Brenda usually fed her. We went back and forth, back and forth, with me patting her back and her still whimpering.

"Don't take it so hard, CP," I told her. "Everybody's gotta puke now and then, but please don't do it again. Neither of us has any more clean clothes to wear. It's winter, and we're not living in a nudist camp."

CP closed her eyes and we continued to glide back and forth. I kept talking to her, hoping the sound of my voice would keep her calm. It was time for her bottle, but I wasn't about to feed her until I was sure her stomach had settled.

"Did I ever tell you about the time in grade school when I puked all over myself and the floor outside the lunchroom? Aw, that was the talk of the third grade for weeks. Your grandma was at work and couldn't come and get me, so Mrs. Sweeney, the school nurse, gave me a clean shirt, wrapped me in a blanket, and then put a cool washcloth on my forehead. She was such a nice lady. She took better care of me than your grandma did, that's for sure. In fact, I came back to school the next day, still sick, 'cuz grandma couldn't afford to take a day off of work, and Mrs. Sweeney not only took care of me, but she'd washed my stinky shirt. I don't think I ever brought back the one she gave me, and she never asked for it, either."

For some reason, remembering the nurse's acts of kindness filled me with a sense of sadness. How many other children had she comforted over the years? She must have provided hundreds of kids with not only exceptional care, but also clean clothes and warm comforting hugs filled with unconditional love.

I don't know what happened to that wonderful woman, but I hoped she was happy and that somehow she knew that her loving care was still appreciated all these years later.

My story must have bored my tiny niece, who'd fallen asleep on my shoulder. I needed to get that laundry done. I could have just eased her back into her crib, but I decided not to. Instead, I sat in the glider for at least another ten minutes going back and forth, holding on to that sweet baby girl, worrying what I would do if she got any sicker.

I was down in the laundry room when the phone rang at nearly eight o'clock. I almost killed myself running up the basement stairs to the kitchen and grabbed it on the fifth ring. "Hello!" I said breathlessly.

"Jeffy?" Brenda asked, sounding worried.

"It's me."

"Why do you sound so winded?"

"I ran all the way from the laundry room to grab the phone."

"What were you doing down there?"

"Washing clothes."

"Oh." She must have figured I was doing my own laundry, as I used their machines on a regular basis. "Is everything okay?"

I hesitated before answering. "Isn't the curtain about to go up?"

"I saw a pay phone when we entered the theater's lobby. You should see this place. It's been beautifully restored to Art Deco perfection."

"Sounds nice."

"I told Richard I was going to the Ladies Room, but I just wanted to see how my three favorite people back home were doing."

"Great," I lied. I wasn't about to spoil her evening. CP had low-grade fevers and puked on a regular basis. All kids did. I could handle her tummy upset.

"Where's Maggie?" Brenda asked.

Again I hesitated before answering. "Probably in the bathroom."

"Again?"

"Hey, when you gotta go, you gotta go."

"Have you given Betsy her nighttime bottle?"

"I was just going to. How's the weather in Toronto?"

"It started to snow as soon as we left the house and it hasn't stopped yet, but tomorrow morning is supposed to be clear. What's it like at home?"

I looked out the window to the dark driveway beyond. Snow was still falling in big clumpy flakes. The plow guy would have to dig us out come morning.

"Could be better," I admitted.

"Good thing you don't have to go anywhere," Brenda said.

"Oh, yeah," I agreed.

"Uh-oh, I think I heard the orchestra start up. I'd better go."

"Enjoy the play," I said.

"Bye," Brenda said, and the connection was broken.

The baby monitor crackled to life once again. CP was back to her fretful cry. I grabbed one of the bottles of breast milk Brenda had left in the fridge, stuck it in the microwave for the precise time she'd indicated on a card she'd left on the counter, and retrieved the bottle. I tested it on my wrist—like I guess everybody does—found it more or less body temperature, and then headed up the stairs.

CP had flipped over from her back to her belly—her latest trick—and was just as cranky as she'd been earlier. I picked her up and sat down on the glider, settling her against my left arm, but when I tried to give her the bottle, she pushed it away.

"It's suppertime. Eat, Betsy, eat," I said, but she wanted nothing to do with the bottle. Instead, she shoved her hand in her mouth, chewing on her fingers.

"Aw, don't do that, CP," I told her, pulling her hand away from her mouth. "You don't know where those fingers have been." But she was not to be deterred. Once again she began to whine. Not a real cry, but a monotone of misery.

I took the baby downstairs to the living room, picked up the TV's remote and hit the power button, then switched to the local news channel for background noise before we began to walk up and down the hall between the grand foyer with its polished marble floor to the parquet floor down the hall to the other end of the house and CP's daddy's study. Back and forth and back and forth. The weather report recycled every ten minutes, telling me what I already knew before it segued into the same boring story about erosion along the shores of Lake Ontario. That got old fast, so I changed the channel and during the next two hours caught fragments of four different couples in various parts of the country searching for their dream homes.

During that time, CP would doze off, drooling against my shoulder. But every time I'd take her back to her crib, she'd wake and begin her miserable cry once more.

"CP, sweetheart, tell Uncle Jeff what's wrong," I pleaded, but her little blue eyes would fill with big wet tears and she'd bury her face in my shoulder once again. Thanks to that damned erratic empathic ability I endured, sometimes CP and I were in sync and sometimes we weren't. Today was one of those non-sync days. I couldn't feel the pain of whatever was bothering her, but I did experience her confusion as well as a general sense of wrongness. She was just a baby—unable to communicate any other way than with tears.

It was almost ten-thirty when we ended up back in the glider once again and CP finally fell into an exhausted sleep. I must have fallen asleep, too, and awoke an hour or so later with a start when CP began to wail in my ear.

I got up, put her on the changing table and gave her a fresh diaper, and then we began to walk the floor again. I'd heard that some sleepless parents bundled their kids up in the back seat of their cars and drove them around for hours at a time, the constant movement helping to get the baby off to sleep. I thought I wasn't prepared to go that far, but after fifteen minutes, CP's cries had only gotten louder and more insistent, and I knew I was in over my head. I needed help—fast—and had no idea where to find it. I considered calling 911 when I suddenly remembered that I did know someone who'd had lots of experience with babies. She'd not only had three children of her own, but five grandchildren—me, among them.

I bundled CP in her lilac-colored snowsuit, grabbed her diaper bag, locked the house, and walked across the snowy driveway to the garage. I unlocked the side door, turned on the light, opened the back door of Brenda's car, then nestled CP into her car seat and buckled her up. CP stuffed her mittened hand into her mouth, squeezed her pretty blue eyes shut, and wailed.

I was never sure if the lights in the closed bakery on Main Street would be on or off when I arrived long after closing time. Sometimes they were, sometimes they weren't. I parked on the side street, extricated a still-teary CP, grabbed the diaper bag, and started off down the sidewalk toward Main Street through ankle-deep snow. Damn. The lights weren't on inside the bakery and I pushed the doorbell feeling more than a little desperate.

CP began to cry again. Big, wet, sad, hopeless sobs of misery and I felt about ready to join her when the lights in the back of the shop snapped on and I saw the bulky silhouetted figure of my psychic mentor, Sophie Levin. Seeing me, she hurried to the door.

"Help!" I said as she held open the door to let us in.

"Is this baby Betsy?" she asked with delight. During the preceding months, I'd brought stacks of pictures of my niece to show her, but never thought I'd have the opportunity to show off CP in person. Unfortunately, the baby wasn't at her best.

"Richard and Brenda went out of town for the night. Maggie was supposed to help me babysit, but caught the flu. Now Betsy's sick and I'm at my wits end. I need your help."

"Come in back," Sophie said, her voice tinged with the hint of a Polish accent, just the sound of it easing my anxiety.

"Get her out of that snowsuit and I'll make cocoa for the two of us."

While she put on a saucepan of water to heat, I unzipped CP and took off her snowsuit, then tossed her over my shoulder, patting her back once more, but she continued to whine inconsolably.

"How long has she been like this?" Sophie asked.

"Since early this afternoon. She's such a good girl. I've never seen her so unhappy. I thought about taking her to the emergency room, but I really don't think she's in any danger. She's just cranky, which isn't like her."

Sophie held out her arms and I passed the baby to her. CP seemed wary, but then Sophie kissed her forehead and she immediately settled down.

"She's got a bit of a fever," I said.

"Not much of one," Sophie said and sat down on one of the folding chairs beside the rickety card table where she usually held court. "You make the cocoa," she told me and bounced CP on her knee.

By the time I returned to the table with two cracked mugs filled with instant hot chocolate, CP had calmed down, but still looked like she might erupt in tears again at any moment.

"Brenda called to check up on the baby around eight tonight. I guess I should have told her CP wasn't feeling well."

"You knew they needed some time alone and you thought you could handle her," Sophie guessed, still bouncing CP on her knee.

"Yeah, but how are they going to feel when I tell them that I lied? That Maggie couldn't come over? That the baby was sick and I didn't know how to help her? They're never going to trust me again."

Sophie frowned. "You are a worry wart."

Didn't she understand how deep in do-do I'd buried

myself?

"It's obvious to me what's wrong."

"Tell me," I begged.

She shook her head as though perturbed. "Come here."

I got up from the table.

"Give me your hand."

I stared at her. "What for?"

"Give me your hand!" she demanded.

I shoved my hand forward. She folded three of my fingers down then guided my index finger toward CP. "Put your finger in her mouth."

"What for?" I again asked.

"Feel her gums. This baby is teething."

I ran my finger along the hard ridges in CP's mouth. There was no sign of a tooth. Her jaws clamped shut and she ground her gums against my finger. It wasn't exactly a pleasant sensation.

"Does Brenda have any teething rings?" Sophie asked.

"Maybe," I said. I didn't even know what a teething ring was.

"They don't cost much. You could get one at the store tomorrow."

It already *was* tomorrow. "There's an all-night pharmacy just down the road. I might be able to get one there," I said as CP continued to chomp on my finger. She seemed less fretful, although she still whined quietly.

"Don't look so worried," Sophie scolded me. "Everybody cuts a first tooth. Maybe by the time Betsy's mama and papa come home tomorrow she can show off hers."

"Maybe," I agreed. I retrieved my finger and went back to the sink to rinse my hands. As I wiped them dry on a linen towel, I looked over my shoulder to take in the sight of Sophie beaming at my tiny niece. Waves of pure happiness seemed to radiate from her.

I sat back down. "When was the last time you held a baby on your lap?"

Sophie's smile was crooked. "When Patty was little."

Patty was my half-sister. Unlike Richard and me, she and I weren't close and I wasn't sure we ever would be. But the mention of her name reminded me that maybe I should at least call her every so often. I owed her that small effort. After all, she had saved my life. Twice.

Sophie held CP's hands and the baby wobbled to raise herself on unsteady legs. "Good girl," Sophie encouraged, her eyes wide with pleasure. CP had no biological connection to my long-dead grandmother, but she was connected to me, and that seemed to be enough for Sophie.

I sipped my cocoa and watched as the old lady played peek-a-boo and other silly games with CP, who actually managed a few brief smiles.

"She's got her daddy's eyes," Sophie commented.

"Yeah," I said. When I looked at that little girl, I sometimes thought my chest would burst from the overwhelming gush of emotion she inspired. I loved that kid as though she were my own. She was an amalgam of the two people I loved most on the planet, and I felt lucky to be a small part of her life.

CP yawned, her eyelids growing heavy.

"Time for you two to go home to bed," Sophie said, her voice tinged with sadness.

"Maybe I can bring her back to visit you some time," I said.

Sophie sighed, but shook her head. She looked across the table at me. "Thank you so much for bringing her here tonight. I never thought I'd ever have the chance to hold a baby again. It's a memory to cherish."

My throat constricted and I looked down at my empty cup.

"Let's get this girl into her snowsuit. You need to get to the store to get what she needs," Sophie said.

Together, we zippered CP into her snowsuit. She looked like a big purple marshmallow. Sophie walked us to the door. "Come and see me again soon," she encouraged.

"I will," I said, and leaned forward to kiss her and we made a sandwich with CP as the filling. The baby giggled, and I knew then that though her gums were still sore, my sweet niece was going to be just fine. "Thanks for being here," I told Sophie.

"I am here for you. I am *only* here for you," she reminded me once again. She clasped my shoulders and turned me and CP toward the door. "Go to the store, then go home and put that child to bed."

"I will," I said once again. "See you soon."

She closed and locked the door after us and then waved from the window.

At least an inch of new snow had fallen since CP and I had entered the bakery. I walked back to the car, buckled her into her car seat, and climbed back behind the wheel. Minutes later, I pulled up to the pharmacy's drive-up window. The woman on duty suggested teething tablets and a couple of teething rings which could be frozen to help numb tender swollen gums. I handed her my Visa card and a minute later we were good to go.

I crossed my fingers and hoped CP and I would get in a few hours of sleep. I had a feeling tomorrow would be a long day—for both of us—before her mom and dad returned home.

Sure enough, Saturday was one of the longest days of my life. I calculated that I had almost four hours of sleep the night before. I don't know how legions of moms kept up with years of working full-time jobs, taking care of their children, and managing a home, because I was exhausted after just one day playing primary caretaker. Still, CP and

I managed to put in a couple of power naps during the day and were good to go for the big reunion.

That evening, CP was buckled into her pink beanbag chair on top of the kitchen table, munching on a teething ring, while I sautéed sausage for the meat sauce I intended to put over a bed of penne pasta. Okay, I'm not much of a cook, and it was a jar of Wegmans garlic-and-basil sauce that would top our meal, but at least Brenda wouldn't have to fuss after a day away and a few hours on the road.

The sky was beginning to darken when Brenda burst in through the back door and into the butler's pantry calling, "We're home." Like I hadn't seen the Mercedes pull into the drive and then the garage a few moments before.

She was immediately drawn to CP and smothered her daughter with kisses as Richard brought up the rear, carrying their big suitcase and a couple of shopping bags which were no doubt filled with toys and new outfits for CP.

"How's my girl?" Richard asked, and CP waved her arms and kicked her feet with joy at the sight of her parents. It made me—her dedicated caregiver for the previous twenty-four hours—feel a little like chopped liver, but … whatever.

Richard and Brenda shucked their coats, and then it was Richard's turn to shower CP with kisses. Brenda took the chair in front of the baby and tugged on her little legs, making the baby giggle.

From Richard's expression, I could see that finding his daughter alive and happy, and his house still intact, had lifted a huge burden from his shoulders. He looked around the kitchen before heading to the liquor cabinet. It was, after all, happy hour. "Where's Maggie?"

Truth time. "She's home."

"Uh-oh. You two aren't fighting, are you?" Brenda asked with concern.

"No, but I doubt I'll be spending much time with her for a few days."

"Why?" Richard asked, taking down the Scotch and bourbon bottles.

"Well, she's got the flu."

"Oh, no!" Brenda said, her eyes suddenly wild with apprehension, and she turned to look at her child. Influenza could be lethal to a baby.

"Don't worry," I said, turning the sausage once again. "Maggie never made it over here."

"But you said she was—"

"Probably in the bathroom—which I assumed she was. Only at *her* house, not yours. I didn't want you guys to worry about only me taking care of CP."

Richard took some ice out from the freezer, plunked it into glasses, and poured us both a drink. "Looks like you guys survived," he said casually, as if his paranoia the day before had never existed.

"Yeah. Maggs called about an hour ago. She's feeling better but is still worried she might be contagious. If nothing else, I'll drop by her place tomorrow with a care package—and then run away fast."

Richard shook his head, smiling.

"What's this?" Brenda asked, picking up one of the new teething rings I'd bought the night before.

"If you stick your finger in her mouth, you'll see CP has a shiny new tooth."

Brenda's mouth drooped. "Oh, no! We missed one of Betsy's first big milestones!"

"If you want to know the truth, it may be a milestone for her, but it wasn't a joyride for me."

Richard handed me a glass. "Oh?"

We'd finished our drinks by the time I'd recounted CP's and my big adventure the night before. I left out all references to Sophie. I wasn't sure they'd understand. By then, the pasta had come to a boil and minutes later was a perfect al dente.

CP and I had gone shopping earlier in the day and had bought a salad and a crusty loaf of Italian bread to go with the rest of the meal. "How did you know we didn't get lunch?" Brenda asked.

"It was a lucky guess," I said, shaking the ice in my glass to hint to Richard that I needed a refill.

Brenda moved CP's beanbag chair to the floor, and then she set the table. Richard opened a bottle of wine and poured, and then the three of us settled down for a nice dinner. CP gummed her teething ring, much happier than she'd been some twenty-four hours before.

"I'm sorry Maggie's sick," Richard said, "but I guess I underestimated you by thinking you needed a backup. You figured out what Betsy needed and you took good care of her." His face seemed to crumple and for a moment I thought he might cry, which I did not want to witness. No doubt his thoughts had harkened back to our troubled past when he'd been forced to play pseudo parent to me ... and hadn't done a very good job. But then, he'd been stretched in far too many directions; saddled with a kid brother he hardly knew, dealing with a stressful job, and trying to referee the disputes that arose between me and his cantankerous grandmother. In retrospect, I think I was far more forgiving of his transgressions than he'd ever be. Over the past twenty-three months we'd become closer than we had ever been during the years we'd lived in the same house. And now we had Brenda and CP, too.

Richard refilled our wineglasses and the three of us clinked them together. "To Betsy Ruth," he proclaimed.

"To Betsy," Brenda echoed.

I glanced down at the floor beside me where CP still gnawed on her teething ring, happily kicking her feet, and I smiled.

It's been two years since the mugging that nearly killed him, and Jeff Resnick is finally putting his life back together. But his sense of peace is shattered when the detective investigating his wife's murder calls to update him on the cold case. Is there a chance Jeff's sixth sense can help him find the man who killed Shelley Resnick?

EYEWITNESS

The phone rang. I'd known it was going to ring. I'd known who was calling. But that didn't make me want to lift the receiver.

I'd received one of those calls every five or six months for the past four years. They were always the same. An apology. A promise to work harder; and reassurance that resolution would one day be at hand.

Yeah. And pigs fly.

I picked up the phone.

"Hello."

"Mr. Resnick? It's Detective Baldwin, NYPD."

"Hi, detective."

"I wanted to update you on your late wife's case."

My late wife. Four years before, Michelle Kathleen Malone Resnick was shot in the back of the head, execution style, in a men's bathroom in Grand Central Terminal after a drug deal gone wrong.

I waited for Baldwin's usual apology.

"We've had a couple of leads," he said instead.

My hand tightened around the receiver. "Oh, yeah?" I managed.

"I don't want you to get your hopes up, but this may be what we've been waiting for."

Yeah, and it might not, either. They'd had leads before that went nowhere. Leads about drug dealers who'd confessed and recanted. About DNA evidence that went nowhere. Fuzzy video that was useless for making an identification. I'd heard it all before.

"What kind of leads?" I asked anyway.

"Testimony in exchange for clemency."

"Yeah? And how's that going?"

"Look, I know you feel jaded by everything that's gone on in the past, but this time it might be the real deal."

I thought about what he said. Every lead they'd ever had had dried up. Every promising tidbit of information had turned out to be false. I was tired of it. I was tired of hearing it. I was tired of Shelley's murder being thrown at me a couple of times a year. The longer it was from the time of her death, the more I should be settled, the less it should affect me. Instead, it was like reopening a serious wound. But maybe there was a chance I could stop it all from erupting all over again. I just had to put my name and reputation on the line to do it.

"Have you ever thought of consulting a psychic to examine the evidence you've collected in the case?"

Baldwin gave a laugh of derision. "Not on your life."

"Would you be open to a psychic talking with you, touching the evidence, and giving you an assessment of what they perceive?"

"Sure, why not?" Baldwin said, his tone flippant. "You got somebody in mind?"

"Yeah. Me."

I didn't want to talk about this in front of my sister-in-law, Brenda, or my girlfriend, Maggie, so I waited a couple of days until I was able to work up the courage to speak to my half-brother, Richard, about it. It was on a Friday afternoon that I found him alone in his study. The room had once belonged to his lawyer grandfather and was a shining example of early twentieth century masculinity. Dark wood and leather dominated, and the bookshelves were filled with tomes the old man had collected long before either Richard or I had been born.

"Hey, Rich, have you got a minute?"

He looked up from his computer screen. "Sure. Sit down."

I plunked down on the leather wing chair in front of the big mahogany desk.

Richard swiveled to face me. "To what do I owe the pleasure?"

I hated asking him for anything. I went out of my way *not* to ask him for anything. It had been that way since I was a teenager, but this was different.

"I'm going to need to borrow some money," I said, not daring to look him in the eye.

"You? Asking for money?" he asked, sounding shocked.

I nodded.

"Then I need a drink."

I looked up just far enough to see him scrutinizing my face. I wouldn't need the money right away; just when my VISA card came due the next month. I didn't like to keep a balance. The interest rates are killer.

"What for?" he asked.

I swallowed. I've got what some might call a sixth sense. I don't read minds; I feel things. I guess you might say I'm empathic and sometimes I know stuff that I couldn't know by any other means. Still, I can't read Richard—and vice versa. But he knows me well. Sometimes I think *too* well. He was still studying my face when it dawned on him.

"Oh, no. Don't tell me you got another call from Detective Baldwin."

"Okay, I won't."

"I thought you said you put all that behind you," he said, worry tinging his voice.

"Yeah, I thought so, too. But I guess I was wrong."

"So, you want the money to go to New York? What for?"

"I...." This was really hard to say. "I sort of offered the detective my services."

Richard's blue eyes widened incredulously. "I wish I'd been a fly on the wall for that conversation. What did he say?"

"He hates having a cold case on his hands. He said..." I paused, remembering an old game-show host's signature line, "to come on down."

Richard stared at the surface of his tidy desk for a long—a very long—time before speaking. "Then I'm coming with you."

"No. I'm not taking you away from Brenda and Betsy—" Richard's wife and five-month old daughter, "—for some idiotic wild goose chase."

"And I won't let you go on your own. You *need* me."

"Rich—" I began.

"No. Really. You need me. Sophie told me so."

It was my turn to look surprised. "What could you possibly know about Sophie?" She was my psychic mentor. A woman who'd been dead for over twenty years.

"I met her."

I shook my head. Sophie had told me on more than one occasion that she was here on this earth for only *me*. Still.... "When?"

"Last year. When Krista Marsh screwed with your head."

I swallowed. Thinking about that time made me sick with shame and self-loathing.

"I went to see her at the bakery," Richard continued.

"And she was there?"

"Just that one time."

Had he gone there other times looking for her?

"What did she look like?" I asked.

"An old, gray-haired lady in a maroon sweater with a hanky stuffed up her sleeve. She's got a cute Polish accent."

That was Sophie all right.

"What did she say?"

"That we were meant to work together. That we're Yin and Yang."

"She said that?" I asked, doubtfully.

Richard shook his head and frowned. "No. She suggested we were more like Laurel and Hardy."

I nodded. I could believe that.

"But the crux was that you need me. That we need each other," Richard said.

Yeah, we do, which hadn't always been true.

"When did you tell Baldwin you'd meet him?" Richard asked.

"Monday morning."

"The last time you flew, you felt like shit afterwards. Why don't we go up Sunday afternoon? That way you'll have some time to recover—in case you need it."

"That's a good idea," I admitted.

"I'll make the arrangements," Richard said.

"I can do it," I protested

Richard shook his head. "I like doing that kind of stuff." He smiled. "You can change Betsy's next messy diaper."

I wrinkled my nose. "If you insist."

"Then it's a deal."

My girlfriend, Maggie, and I had been together for almost two years. Sort of. I'd met her just about two years before, just after her ex-boss had been killed, and on our first real date we kind of discovered his wife, who had also been murdered and … well, it was all a bit of a mess. It had taken us another three months to figure out if we wanted to pursue a relationship. I knew I did. Maggie wasn't quite as sure.

As a couple, we'd certainly had our ups and downs. Like ten months before when Maggie dumped me for her former fiancé—until he'd shown himself to be a heel for a second time. And then, her good friend and ex-mother-in-law had had a stroke, which had kept Maggie busy taking care of the old lady, who also happened to live in the bottom half of Maggie's duplex.

Yeah. We'd had lots more downs than ups. So it was with apprehension that I dared mention my late wife's name. The truth was, Shelley and I had called it quits six months before her murder, but part of me had never stopped hoping that she'd come back to me. That she'd find the strength to give up her drug habit and we could resume our lives together—that we'd buy that little house in New Jersey and raise a family. I'd been stupid to hope against hope.

Shelley had left me and taken most of our assets with her. I was broke when she was murdered. But I was her next of kin. I went into hock to pay for her funeral and I promised myself that that was the end of my commitment to Shelley.

I'd been wrong. I'd lied to myself. After four years, it got so I didn't think of Shelley on a daily basis, but if I was honest with myself, she was never really all that far from my thoughts. I considered her my biggest failure because despite my best efforts, I couldn't save her from herself.

I won't say that Maggie was jealous of her predecessor, but Shelley had become a sore subject—one we rarely spoke of. There'd been that one—and only—time when Maggie and I were both a little drunk and were making love, and I'd whispered Shelley's name into Maggie's ear. She had never really forgotten that. And, in fact, that one event had set us on a path where we'd broken up for a while. Of course, relationships are built—and destroyed—on more than one incident. We'd been working hard to get past all that, but almost a year later, things were still a little strained.

So it was with trepidation that I brought up the subject the evening before Richard and I were to leave for New York. Maggie had come for dinner at my place, and I hoped to stay the night. And yet, I also knew that wasn't a given. Maggie hadn't had to say a word for me to know that all was not right in her world, either.

"I need to tell you something, Maggs," I said as I poured her a glass of wine. She sat on one of the stools in front of the breakfast bar in my apartment over the garage on Richard's property.

"I knew something was up," she said, sounding wary. "Give it to me straight."

"Richard and I are going to New York tomorrow."

"What for?" she asked sounding suspicious. She knew Richard wouldn't leave his wife and baby for anything trivial.

"It seems there have been some developments in Shelley's murder case."

Maggie accepted the wineglass I handed her and took a hearty swig before speaking. "Like what?"

"Jailhouse testimony."

"And how reliable is that?" she asked, an edge creeping into her voice.

"I don't know. But it finally occurred to me that if I could examine the evidence—maybe talk to the guy, and anybody else who says they have knowledge about the circumstances of her death—that this whole thing could be cleared up and I would never have to think about it again."

"Ya think?" she asked, sounding skeptical, maybe even a little bitter.

"Whether I like it or not, I seem to have this stinking psychic-empathic ability. The idea of confronting Shelley's death—maybe actually experiencing it—isn't something I'd normally seek out, but I'm fucking tired of it hanging over me. It hangs over us, Maggs. It's got to stop, and there's only one way I can think of to make that happen."

Maggie's lower lip trembled. "And so you and Richard are going to New York?"

I nodded.

She let out a pent-up breath. "I won't pretend to be happy to hear about this. I'd like nothing better than to finally rid that bitch from both our lives, but are you sure that's likely to happen?"

She had a lot of nerve asking that of me when, the previous year, she'd been content to once again take up with a guy who had humiliated her years before and, more recently, had been willing to sell her off when the going got tough.

I answered honestly. "I don't know. But I hope so."

Maggie wouldn't look at me. She clasped the wineglass so hard I thought it might shatter. "It doesn't matter what I say or think. You've already made up your mind to go."

"Yeah, I have."

Maggie shook her head and her eyes welled with tears, and she broadcast a myriad of confusing emotions—fear and dread topping the list.

I frowned. "I don't get it. You can't be jealous of Shelley. She's dead."

"Yeah, and she still takes up a really big space in your heart."

"No more than your ex-husband does for you. You've told me you've forgiven him. Hell, you even accepted the fact that he married the guy he left you for. Why can't you cut me the same slack?"

"I don't know. Maybe because I'm worried about how what you find out could affect you. You like to think of yourself as all healed from the crap you endured with Shelley, and then the mugging, but you're not. You're really pretty fragile."

I considered what she'd said. Yeah. Back in May I was pretty much a basket case. But I'd healed. I'd grown stronger. My family ties were better than they'd ever been. Maggie's and my relationship had been the weak link in the chain, but I'd thought we'd gotten through the worst of things. Why did she want to rehash the crap of the past?

"I'm looking for closure. Nothing more."

"Oh, yeah? You who have made contact with the spirit world before?"

Had I? Or had I dreamed—or worse, hallucinated—about connecting with those previously alive?

But then Richard had had a supernatural experience, too. I didn't want to think about it. Still, I needed to address Maggie's concerns.

"Oh, Babe. You have nothing to be concerned about when it comes to my feelings for Shelley. She screwed me. She ruined me financially. She robbed me of everything I held dear."

"And yet you still feel compelled to find whoever killed her. Why?"

I had to think about it. I had to swallow down the huge lump that had formed in the back of my throat. "Because I once vowed to love her in sickness and in health. Her drug addiction was a terrible sickness."

"What about the *'til death do you part* piece of that equation? Because she's now dead. You've been forever parted. Or have you?"

"How could I connect with her? I'm here in Buffalo— nearly four hundred miles away."

"Well, you won't be if you go to Manhattan."

"She's buried in New Jersey."

"Which isn't all that far from where you'll be."

Maggie was talking nonsense. Then again, I remembered a scene from the movie Ghostbusters that I'd seen a million years before on TV. Where one of the spirit eradicators had been seduced by a sexy apparition. Did Maggie think I was into necrophilia? Shelley had not been embalmed. Did Maggie think I would be attracted to a moldering corpse? Now I was delving into horror—or dark fantasy. Either way, I didn't want to think about it.

"Maggs, you're being unreasonable."

She pursed her lips before speaking. "Maybe. But I can't help the way I feel." Maggie pushed her still half-full wineglass forward.

"You're not going to stay tonight, are you?" I asked, disappointed.

"No."

I guess I should have expected that answer. "Do you want me to call you when I come home?"

She shrugged. "I guess."

Why didn't I just open the silverware drawer and hand her a butcher knife, because her words had pierced my heart like a wicked attack. She knew it, too. But I wasn't nasty enough to throw it in her face. She'd been scarred by betrayal too many times to fully trust. I understood that. She didn't trust me now, but I knew I'd come back to Buffalo and our bond could only grow stronger. But for now, I had to listen and accept that she was afraid.

I moved around my breakfast bar and stood before her. "I love you, Maggs. I get where you're coming from, but I need to do this. It's going to be awful. It's going to wound my soul. But if I'm lucky, I'll lay Shelley to rest once and for all. I know you don't want to hear this, but she was my first real love. We were happy together for far too short a time. She screwed me. But I vowed for better and for worse. I'm still bound by that promise."

Maggie shook her head. "I wouldn't respect you if you

weren't. But this is really hard—especially right now."

I stepped forward and wrapped my arms around her. "I know," I said, but I really wasn't sure what she meant. Both our emotions were so conflicted that I felt a tremendous sense of turmoil.

She hugged me back, and I absorbed the painful, conflicting emotions that swirled within her. Still, I hugged her tighter, and she did likewise.

"I'm sorry," she whispered in my ear.

"Shhh. It's okay."

We clung together for a long time, but finally Maggie pulled back. "I have to go home."

I nodded. "Can I call you while I'm gone?"

She managed a wan smile. "I'll be pissed if you don't."

"I *will* come home. You, and Richard, and Brenda, and Betsy are my family. But I need to get through this and put it behind me."

"I understand," Maggie said, but I knew she didn't. She stood, and I followed her to the closet where she'd hung up her coat when she'd first arrived. I grabbed it and helped her into the sleeves.

"Call me when you get home. Just so I don't worry. If you don't want to talk, just give me the old double-ring ceremony," I said. Two rings and she'd hang up. We'd done this so many times in the past.

"I will," she promised.

I kissed her on the nose. Then I kissed her lips. I kissed her again and again. "I love you, Maggs."

"I love you, too," she said.

I didn't doubt it. Sometimes, like now, she still did.

"Will you call me tomorrow night?" she asked.

"You bet."

She nodded and turned for the stairs that led to the driveway. I watched her go, then closed the door and moved to the window in my living room. She got in her car and drove away.

Maggie was worried about what I'd learn about my ex-wife and the circumstances of her death and how I'd feel about it.

She wasn't the only one.

The flight from Buffalo to the Big Apple took just about an hour and was pleasant for everyone on board. Everyone except me, that is. Stuffed in a metal tube—with engines roaring on both sides of the plane—made me feel claustrophobic, and the emotional baggage of seventy or eighty other people was painful to endure. I was glad Richard had come along. I needed a keeper after I stumbled off the plane. He dragged me to the luggage carousel, parked me against a support pillar, and retrieved our bags.

"Can you get us a cab?" I asked, my eyes scrunched to half-mast to keep out the worst of the fluorescent light.

"No cab," he said and pointed toward a bearded guy in a black overcoat with a black cap holding a sign up that said ALPERT. "We're traveling by limo."

"Limo?" I asked. "Why?"

"Because we can."

I sometimes forget that Richard is filthy rich.

We met up with the driver, who immediately took charge of the luggage and led us to a black Lincoln Town Car. We eased into the backseat, buckled up, and I sank back, closing my eyes and hoped the pounding in my skull would miraculously abate.

The ride from the airport to the city seemed to take forever. If I hadn't felt so lousy, I might have watched the scenery go by, anticipating familiar landmarks. I'd lived in Manhattan for almost fourteen years, most of them unhappy. But this wasn't a pleasure trip, I had to remind myself.

Finally the car pulled up to a curb and the driver got out.

"We're here," Richard said.

I sat up straighter and looked around, trying to get my bearings. We weren't in front of any hotel I knew. "Where are we?"

"At our destination," Richard said obliquely.

I unbuckled my seat belt and got out of the car. The luggage was waiting on the sidewalk. Richard tipped the driver, who gave a nod and got back into the car, pulling away. I tilted my head back until it hurt, looking up at the building that seemed to be totally clad in black glass. I didn't have time to ask any other questions as Richard had picked up our bags and started for the front door. I shouldered deeper into the new heavy coat I'd bought for the trip and followed him. A doorman stood ready to welcome us.

The lobby was a sea of gray tile and black granite. A man in his early thirties, dressed in a black suit and blue tie, with a crisp white shirt, sat behind the reception desk. "Good afternoon, gentlemen. How can I help you?"

"I'm Richard Alpert."

"Ah, yes," the man said and reached for something. He handed Richard an envelope. "If you need anything, please feel free to call down. The number is printed on the card inside."

"Thank you," Richard said. He turned to me. "The elevators are just over here."

I followed him, wondering where the hell he was taking me.

Richard pressed the *up* button and, magically, the elevator doors opened. We got in. Richard hit the button for the eleventh floor.

"I take it you know where we're going."

"I've been here before," he said.

Since we weren't in a hotel, this had to be a swanky apartment building. "I didn't know you owned a place here in Manhattan."

"I don't."

Before I could ask for clarification, the elevator came to a halt and the doors opened. Richard strode into the hallway, turning left. I followed him to a door marked 1104. He took a keycard from the envelope, slid it into a slot, and the lock clicked. He opened the door, leading the way, and flipped a light switch. I closed the door behind us. "I'm confused. Are you borrowing a friend's apartment?"

"Sort of," he said, and set the bags down. He unbuttoned his coat. To his left was a closet, where he hung his coat and waited for mine, then hung it, too. "Come on inside," he said, leaving the bags on the entry's marble floor. He walked into the darkened living room and turned on a number of lamps. He obviously knew this place well.

"Give," I said, taking in the comfortable contemporary furnishings that leaned to leather and chrome.

Richard took one of the chairs, inviting me to do the same. He kicked off his shoes. "This apartment is owned by the foundation I use to work for in Pasadena."

"The place that let you and Brenda go?" I asked.

He nodded.

"Why would they let you use the place gratis?"

"Because the guy who runs the foundation and I are still good friends. He fought to keep Brenda and me, and he lost."

"Your friend, Michael?" I guessed.

Richard nodded. "This apartment sits empty most of the year. Knowing the way you absorb the residual auras of people, and how detrimental it can be, I didn't want to park you in a hotel. I wanted us to stay in a quiet place without a lot of baggage attached to it."

"I appreciate that," I said. I took a deep breath. There weren't any discernable emotions in the apartment. The people who had stayed there came with a purpose, fulfilled their obligations, and left. "It feels pretty tranquil." That said, my head still pounded. "I'm sorry to be such a wet blanket, but I need to crash."

Richard stood. "Come on. The bedrooms are just down the hall. Do you want the master?"

I shook my head—wincing. It was his connection that had brought us here. I was more than willing to let him have the better bedroom.

Richard led the way, entering the room and turning on the bedside light.

The second bedroom turned out to be bigger and a lot nicer than my own back in Buffalo. The apartment had to be worth a couple million dollars or more in a city where square footage came at a premium. Hell, my entire former apartment could have fit in that beautiful living room alone.

Richard drew back the bedspread. "Take a nap. You'll feel better later."

He left me and it was my turn to kick off my shoes.

I turned off the light and climbed onto the bed. Since it had been so long since anyone had slept on the mattress, I glommed onto nothing at all.

I closed my eyes and slept.

The hall light was on when I awoke, and from somewhere in the distance I could hear the soft strains of Vivaldi's Four Seasons—Richard's favorite piece of music. He listened to it over and over again. It was cheerful—at least the part I was most familiar with. Cheerful seemed to equal hope. Unfortunately, the only hope this little trip offered me was an opportunity to put an end to the calls and distressing interruptions in my life.

My head was no longer pounding, which was good. But my gut felt tight. Whatever I learned in the next day or so would be painful and bring up nothing but unhappy memories. The sting of failure was still sharp because I hadn't been able to help Shelley during those last miserable months of her existence. If my efforts could help discover the person or persons who'd stolen her life, it would at least let me finally put that part of my life behind me forever.

I found Richard in the living room consulting his iPad. He looked up as I entered. "Oh, good, you're awake. Come and sit. How are you feeling?"

"Much better." I took the seat opposite him. The drapes were open and night had fallen. The lights in the surrounding buildings looked like something out of a travel brochure. I nodded toward the stereo. "Vivaldi."

"I plugged in my iPod," he said simply. "Is it too early for me to ask about tomorrow?"

I shook my head. "We're supposed to see Detective Baldwin at eight."

"Are you ready for what you might experience?"

"I don't know. But I'd like to finally put that chapter of my life with Shelley behind me. Maybe then Maggie and I can finally move forward."

Richard looked away. That had to mean something. His wife was Maggie's best friend. Had Maggie confided to Brenda—who'd shared with my brother—her true feelings about our relationship where she hadn't spoken of it to me the night before? I wasn't sure how I felt about that possibility. And I wasn't about to voice my misgivings to Richard. At least not then.

A glass of what looked like Scotch sat before him on the chrome-and-glass cocktail table. "Is there anything here I might like to drink?"

Richard smiled. "While you were asleep, I visited a liquor store and a deli. I wasn't sure if you'd want to go out, so I got some stuff that should stave off starvation tonight and for breakfast tomorrow."

"Good idea. Thanks."

"The bourbon's on the counter in the kitchen. Want me to fix you a drink?"

I shook my head. "I can do it." I got up and headed for the kitchen. The decor wasn't unlike the lobby, and was also finished in gray tile and black granite counters. I found a bottle of club soda in the fridge and poured myself a drink before heading back to the living room. I sat down and took a sip. Richard's gaze seemed riveted on the area rug beneath the couch and cocktail table. There was something on his mind.

"Did Brenda say anything to you these past couple of days about Maggie and me?" I asked.

"No."

I wasn't sure I believed him.

"Maggie's pissed at me. She thinks I'm going to connect with Shelley in some kind of kinky way."

He looked up. "You're kidding."

I shrugged. "I don't understand her concern, but yeah, she's freaked."

He shook his head and changed the subject. "I don't want to get in your way tomorrow, but if things get too intense, I'm going to shut this whole thing down—at least so you can recoup enough to try again."

"I'm not looking forward to it, but it's got to be done."

Richard nodded. "Do you realize that two days from now is the anniversary of our mother's death?"

"Yeah. I hate the month of March. Nothing good ever happens."

"It was two years ago this week that you came back into my life. I think that's something to celebrate."

It would never have happened if I hadn't nearly lost my life at the hands of a couple of baseball bat-wielding thugs but, yeah, he had a point.

"Let's drink to that, if nothing else," Richard said.

And so we did.

We arrived at the police station at seven fifty-five the next morning. We'd had coffee and toasted a couple of almost-stale bagels, slathering them with cream cheese before we'd left the apartment, but we hadn't spoken much. I didn't know what to say. Likewise, my call to Maggie the night before had been brief with lots of things left unsaid.

Though I'd spoken with Detective Baldwin on a number of occasions, I'd never met him in person. Because his surname was Baldwin, I guess I'd associated him with the actor Alec Baldwin, but he looked nothing like the big, charismatic guy. Instead, the police detective was rather short and thin, his gray hair thinning. He also sported a colorful bow tie, which was kind of unsettling, although I couldn't have explained why. We shook hands and I got no kind of psychic signature from him, which was a tremendous relief.

"This is my brother, Dr. Richard Alpert," I said.

Baldwin and Richard shook hands before the detective turned back to me. "I did as you asked and contacted Detectives Hayden and Wilder back in Buffalo. They seem to think you're the real deal."

Thank you, Carl and Bonnie, I thought.

"If they hadn't spoken so highly of you, we wouldn't be having this conversation right now."

"I won't mislead you. Sometimes I get stuff and sometimes I don't. If I get nothing from what you've got to show me, I won't bullshit you. I'll go home and that will be the end of it."

"It's been my experience that psychics are fakes—charlatans," Baldwin said.

I gave him a wan smile. "That's been my experience, too."

"I've got things set up in a conference room down the

hall. Follow me, please."

We traipsed behind him to the small, stark room with a big glass mirror on one of the walls. Conference room my ass. It was an interrogation room. But I doubted anyone was behind the two-way mirror on that morning.

Baldwin indicated that we should sit, and he took his own seat at the head of the table. He reached behind him and grabbed a clear plastic bag, which he plopped onto the top of the ugly gray steel-and-Formica table. "These are the clothes your wife was wearing when she was murdered."

I studied the jumbled mass of cloth in the bag. "I have to touch them to get anything. Would that be okay?"

"They're considered a biohazard."

"I'm not worried about it."

"Then be my guest," Baldwin said and sat back in his chair. He looked at me as though I was just some asshole con man who'd walked in off the street. I had no street cred with him, despite what Detectives Hayden and Wilder had told him. Well, who could blame him? And if I got nothing from the clothes then Richard and I would just go home and I'd have to live with the fact that I might never get the closure I sorely craved.

I opened the bag, pulling out a blood-stained blouse. As soon as I touched it, my breaths came fast and ragged, and I sensed the vast, torrential nothingness of death. I rubbed the fabric between my left thumb and forefinger and experienced a tidal wave of fear. I closed my eyes and suddenly I *was* Shelley, and scared shitless. My mind seemed to be caught in a loop: terrified and gone, terrified and gone, terrified and gone.

My eyes welled with tears, but they weren't Shelley's—they were mine. My beautiful Shelley—just a husk of who she had been—had been petrified in the seconds before her life was snuffed out like a cheap candle. Luckily she'd died before the pain could register and then there was the total oblivion of death.

I dropped the cloth as though I'd been burned.

"What are you feeling?" Richard asked dispassionately.

"Just her death. Not who or what was behind it," I said, still fighting tears.

"Well, that's not helpful," Baldwin said dully.

I turned a murderous glare in his direction.

"Calm down," Richard told me. "Take out another piece of clothing. See if you get anything else."

It took all my courage to do just that. The next thing I pulled out of the bag was a pair of pink nylon panties Shelley had worn the day she'd died. A terrible wave of recollection passed through me. Shelley had let the bastard who'd killed her essentially rape her. She expected a powerful, euphoric fix from the guy. She had fallen so far from the woman I had known and loved, thinking so little of herself. Why hadn't she let me help her redefine her sense of self? Yet somehow I knew that she hadn't wanted her life to spiral out of control, but once she was hooked on smack, she had to endure whatever it took to get a fix. The thing was, the guy had worn a condom. I got the idea that he figured a stinking little junkie like Shelley was likely to give him an STD and he wasn't willing to take the chance.

I tossed the panties aside, my eyes again welling with tears and suddenly Richard was standing over me. He put a hand on my shoulder. "It's okay."

Yeah. The moment Shelley's underwear had left my grasp things *were* better.

I took a shuddering breath before speaking. "Shelley had sex with the guy who killed her."

"There was no DNA evidence to prove that."

"He flushed the spent condom. This guy was smart and had probably planned his every move in advance."

"Do you get a sense of who it was who killed Shelley?" Richard asked.

Unfortunately, I didn't. I shook my head.

"Do you need to touch any more of the clothes?" he asked.

Again I shook my head. "I don't think I'm going to get anything else of worth from them." I turned to look at Detective Baldwin. "What else have you got in the way of evidence?"

"Some spent shells."

"Can I touch one of them?"

"It's okay by me. We found no fingerprints or DNA on them." He handed me a plastic bag.

I opened it and touched one of the shell casings. Immediately a Russian—Ukrainian, and Polish—phrase came to mind. *Nastrovia.* It was spelled differently, depending on which language it was spoken in, but essentially it meant the same thing: *To your health.* Yeah, not funny, considering the bullets had delivered death. *Nastrovia.* Half my family was Polish. I'd heard that phrase many times when I'd been far too young to know what it meant. The person who'd thought the phrase as he'd loaded the gun was definitely Russian.

"The guy who killed my wife was Russian, or at least of Russian descent."

Baldwin's expression darkened. "That's what we think, too. How did you know?"

I shrugged. "I just do. But I don't have anything concrete … like a name or a face. Just a word."

"But … how?" he asked again in disbelief.

"I don't know how I know stuff. I just do. You've obviously got an idea of where to look for this guy. You mentioned a jailhouse confession."

"Not a confession; jailhouse testimony for leniency."

"And is the guy Russian?"

"No," Baldwin said. "But the man he implicated is."

"Any chance I can talk to your source?"

"I can arrange for it to happen tomorrow."

"Let's do that," I said.

He nodded.

"In the meantime, I'd like to see the surveillance video you've got."

"Can do," Baldwin said. "I should have brought it with me. It's back on my desk. I'll be right back." He left us.

Richard turned to me. "You're doing really well."

That was a matter of opinion.

"We're going to have hours to kill this afternoon while Baldwin makes arrangements for us to see the witness. How would you like to spend it?"

"I need to go where Shelley died; Grand Central Terminal."

"Are you sure?" Richard asked, sounding doubtful.

I nodded. "But I don't need an NYPD guided tour. After we watch the video, I'll know where I need to go and what I need to look for."

Richard nodded. "Whatever you say."

Though I can't read Richard at all, I guessed he had something else on his mind. "Is there somewhere *you'd* like to go while we're here?"

He looked sheepish. "A toy store. I'd like to bring home something special for Betsy."

"Don't do it," I told him flatly.

"What? You don't think I should bring my daughter a present from my trip?"

"Rich, Betsy's a baby. The only thing she cares about right now is chomping on a teething ring. You've got years and years ahead of you to spoil her. Wait until it will count."

"I guess you're right," he said, but I also guessed what else he was thinking. He'd left his wife and baby girl *alone and he felt guilty about it—which made* me feel guilty about it, too.

"What about Brenda? Am I allowed to buy *her* a present?" he asked.

Somehow, I managed a smile. "Well, at least she can appreciate it."

That seemed to satisfy him. He smiled, and I wondered if a little blue box from Tiffany's might come home with him.

"What else should we do this afternoon?" he asked.

"If you don't mind, I'd like to walk around my old neighborhood. Maybe visit my old watering hole."

"Is that a good idea?" Richard asked, again sounding worried.

"Why not? I left the city with my whole life in flux. I'd kind of like to put that behind me, too."

Richard's gaze dropped to focus on the crummy table in front of us. "Are you ever sorry I dragged you back to Buffalo?"

I thought about the question before answering. "Sometimes, in the early days ... yeah. But then we finally got to be friends, and I met Maggie, and now with Betsy's arrival—I can't think of anywhere else I'd rather be."

Richard let out a breath and seemed to deflate a little. "I'm glad you feel that way."

"I'm not saying Buffalo is paradise, but it's where I need to be right now." And probably for the rest of my life. That said, I hate winter. I hate the snow, the cold, and the relentless wind. But as long as Richard, Brenda, Betsy, and Maggie were there, it was the only place on Earth I wanted to be.

We both looked up as Baldwin approached, came into the room, and settled a disc into the player under a TV that sat on a rolling cart.

"You don't want to watch an hour of raw video. This has been condensed to show the highlights."

Shelley's murder was considered a highlight?

"Your wife showed up in the grand concourse at about one in the morning, moving to stand under the clock."

I knew that location very well. The antique four-sided clock was the multi-million dollar jewel of the cavernous commuter train station. Lots of people met there. Hell, I'd met a bunch of women there when on blind dates before and after my time with Shelley, but things had never worked out.

I'd been honest with Maggie when I'd told her that Shelley was my first love. I'd worked two jobs during my high school years and nobody had been interested in dating a nerd like me. The truth was, my first sexual experience was with a hooker in a parking lot in San Francisco on my first leave from the Army. I found the experience empty and disappointing, and it was pure luck I didn't get an STD. After that, I dated a lot of women, but never had a satisfying relationship until I'd met Shelley. And while I'd loved her with all my heart, it wasn't as good—or meaningful—as my best times with Maggie.

I was a stupid kid of fifteen when Richard had told me—in a moment when he'd first offered me, and I'd rejected, his hand in friendship—that we were both emotional cripples. That neither of us knew how to love or be loved. His assessment had been right on the money. Oh, if only I could have gone back to that day and listened to his words, and changed my reaction ... maybe we'd both have lived different lives. But we were where we were, and after way too many unhappy years we were both now pretty much content. That had to be worth something.

I had to shake myself to tune back into the present and concentrate on what Baldwin had said. "Hit play," I told him.

He did, and the screen came to life. The camera must have been mounted somewhere on the ceiling. A figure walked across the empty concourse and stood under the big clock. Seconds ticked by. Long, long seconds. You could see by the hair and clothes that the figure was a woman, but real identification wasn't actually possible. I had to take Baldwin's word that the woman on the screen had been Shelley.

Eventually, another figure in a long dark coat approached. The man and woman spoke for thirty or forty seconds and then the man grabbed the woman's arm and steered her off screen. The video had obviously been edited and the camera angle changed, again showing the man, grasping the woman's arm, and steering her off to one side. I knew where they'd gone. The men's room. There were no cameras there. The video played for two or three minutes with no sign of either of them, then the man came back out, hunched inside his long dark coat, his head down, his features undiscernible.

The video continued to play for another few minutes before another figure showed up, heading for the men's room. Too soon, the figure darted out into the main concourse, obviously agitated, with cell phone in hand—no doubt reporting Shelley's lifeless body in one of the stalls.

The video ended.

Baldwin turned off the machine and retrieved the disk. He sat back down. "Well?"

I shook my head. The worst was yet to come. "Can I see the crime scene photos?"

"Aw, Jeff, are you sure you want to do that?" Richard asked, his distress obvious.

I steeled myself. "I was an insurance investigator for a lot of years," I told Baldwin—no doubt a fact he was well aware of. "Crime scenes were once my specialty."

Yeah, they were … until Shelley had been killed, and then I'd asked for a transfer to the fraud unit. My new supervisor and I hadn't hit it off, and eighteen months later I'd been let go. I wasn't enough of a team player for him. The prick.

"They're pretty grim," Baldwin said.

"I never saw a crime scene that wasn't," I commented, my voice sounding a lot calmer than I felt.

Again Baldwin reached behind him and produced a fat file folder. He handed it to me.

The photos were all in vivid color. Shelley—my wife—had been reduced to just a crime victim. She lay face down on the tile floor beside a gleaming porcelain toilet. The back of her skull was a dark gooey brown mass. Her blood had already oxidized by the time the photos had been taken, hours after her death. Again and again, I swallowed hard as I paged through the photos.

Most of the shots were taken from overhead, or from a distance of a couple of feet. Only a few of them were sidelong shots of her face, some rigid and some lax in death. They weren't pretty. The person in the pictures bore only a slight resemblance to the woman I'd known and loved, but I feared that I'd see those pictures again and again in my dreams for a long time to come.

I looked away, covered my mouth with my hand, and let out a long, shuddering breath. Again, Richard was suddenly standing over me. "You don't have to do this."

Unfortunately … I did.

I shuffled though the photos once again, trying not to look at the body as someone I'd been intimately acquainted with and loved. This time I looked at the blood splatter pattern. Yeah, she'd been killed execution style. And then things got clearer.

"It wasn't vaginal sex. The guy who killed her was a back-door man. And at the height of his excitement—" the bastard had ridden poor Shelley like a bucking bronco, "he pulled out the gun and shot her."

But that wasn't all. "She'd paid him for the drugs with cash—and God only knows where she got it. Probably stole it—but he demanded more. To get what she needed, she'd acquiesced. The bastard had taken her money, raped her, and then killed her."

My fingers curled so tight around the photos I began to crush them.

Richard eased around me and snatched them from my grasp. "That's enough."

He was right. I'd seen more than enough for one day.

I swallowed—again and again—and the details played and replayed through my mind. The blood splatters on the tile. The remnants of brain and bone. The sad shot of Shelley's curled fingers, the nails clad in chipped red polish. Yet, on her left ring finger was the gold band I'd placed there on our wedding day. It had been returned to me, but I'd given it back to the undertaker and Shelley had been buried wearing it.

Despite all her lows—all the drugs she'd needed to buy—she hadn't hocked the ring.

Until that moment, that fact hadn't registered in my grief-stricken brain.

Maybe she had actually loved me after all.

We didn't take a cab to my old neighborhood. Instead, we walked. And walked. And walked. I needed the time to recover from the things I'd seen and felt and was grateful Richard didn't push for conversation. Everything looked so achingly familiar, and yet totally alien to me. The neighborhood had once been home, but now it wasn't. We stopped in front of my former apartment building. I looked up at windows I'd so often looked out. Someone else had lived there for the past two years. I hoped they were happier than I'd been between those walls.

"I never saw the apartment after it was ransacked," I said to Richard.

"I'm glad of that. It wasn't pretty," he admitted. "Do you want to go inside?"

I shook my head. "No reason to. It's almost

lunchtime. Let's go to O'Shea's. Maybe somebody there will still remember me."

So we headed south down the sidewalk, which was crowded with people. No matter the time of day or night, there never seemed to be a sidewalk in New York that wasn't filled with people. I hadn't noticed before, but despite the mass of humanity, the bustle of the city left me feeling terribly empty—probably because I had no connection with any of them. In all the years I'd lived in that teeming metropolis, I'd only ever really connected with one other person: Shelley.

"Where is this bar?" Richard asked.

"Just a couple of blocks away."

We bucked the oncoming pedestrian traffic when all of a sudden I stopped dead in the middle of the sidewalk. The guy behind me crashed into me and swore, then darted around me. Richard kept walking. He hadn't noticed I'd lagged behind.

I had to swallow a few times and backed up to stand against the plate glass window of a deli. The last time I'd seen the place, it was shrouded in darkness with a locked cage keeping it safe from robbers and vandals. Across the way was a bakery. An OPEN sign flashed in green-and-white neon. It, too, had been dark the last time I'd seen it. The night of the mugging. The night I'd nearly died.

Richard had finally noticed I'd stalled in neutral and backtracked to join me. "Are you okay?"

I nodded. "This is the spot."

"Spot?"

"This is where I had my head caved in."

Richard's expression darkened. He looked all around, then back at me. "Are you okay?" he asked again.

I took a deep breath and seemed to shrink within my new heavy winter coat. "Yeah." The truth was, the flashbacks of that terrible night had pretty much faded since October, when I'd been forced to face my fears. That was when a young black man had come to stay as Richard's houseguest just before Betsy had been born. I'd been mugged by a couple of young black guys. Da-Marr and I hadn't hit it off. In fact, the kid's presence had freaked me out. But we'd kind of bonded when we'd nearly died out on the Niagara River. A few days later, he'd returned to Philadelphia. Now, we were Facebook friends and traded jokes, likes, and shares.

"They never found the guys who hurt you," Richard reminded me.

"Yeah, well, I'm pretty much done with dwelling on it." I gave myself a shake. "I'm more interested in visiting O'Shea's. Come on."

We waited for a break, then jumped back into the long line of walkers and continued on our way. It felt like I'd accomplished some monumental feat by not having a meltdown. The wound from that experience had finally scabbed over and was starting to heal. I felt pretty good about that—and after what I'd been through just an hour or so before, it seemed like progress.

As we approached the cross street, I could already see that the bar I had once loved must have changed hands, as the name above the bank of beveled glass windows was different. It was now called Lady Liberty, with a picture of the Lady of the Harbor as their icon.

We paused at the curb, waiting for the light to change.

"That's your old neighborhood bar?" Richard asked skeptically.

"No, it's not. It used to be an Irish pub."

"No shepherd's pie or bangers-and-mash for lunch," Richard predicted.

The light changed and we crossed the street.

We strode to the front of the bar and I plunged ahead, opening the door and entering. Once inside, I stopped dead as at least twenty women turned to glare at me and Richard, and I quickly realized we'd just invaded a lesbian haven.

"We're not in Kansas anymore," Richard muttered only loud enough for me to hear.

"Welcome, gentlemen. What can we do for you?" asked the woman behind the bar. Her dusky red hair had been shorn in what used to be called a brush cut. Her forearms were decorated with tattoos, and her ears and nose were pierced more than once. She proudly wore a Syracuse University sweatshirt with the sleeves pushed up.

"Hi," I said, walking up to the old oak bar I used to know so well, but the rest of the décor had radically changed. The place used to be dark, with lots of golden oak wood and splashes of green, along with horse brass, Celtic crosses, and the occasional shamrock. All that had been obliterated and the walls were now a stark white with a plethora of black-and-white photos of women of substance decorating the walls: Susan B. Anthony, Betty Freidan, Gloria Steinham, and even Elizabeth Warren. "Got any Canadian on tap?"

The woman shook her head. "Sorry. Sam Adams?" she offered.

"That'll do," I said.

"Make that two," Richard chimed in.

She drew two brews as we commandeered a couple of seats at the bar.

"Let me guess," the bartender said. The nametag she wore or her shirt said Maggie. How apropos. "You used to come here when this place was O'Shea's."

"Damn straight."

She laughed. "You're not the first."

"What happened?" I asked, taking out a twenty and laying it on the bar.

"The way I hear it, one of the waitresses got deported."

"Annie?" I guessed.

She nodded. "The owner was so bummed he closed the joint and followed her back to Dublin."

"That's nice," I said and smiled. "Did they get married?"

She shrugged. "I have no idea." She made change, set it before me, and turned back to her regular patrons.

"Who was Annie?" Richard asked, taking a sip of his beer.

A warm smile of remembrance crept onto my lips. "She was special. A real sweetheart. I wanted to date her—and she was receptive—but I was broke. I was too timid to court her when it was a stretch for me to pay for a couple of beers for myself every week. If she ended up with Ian, she couldn't have found anyone better."

"And now you've got your own Maggie in your corner."

I leveled an inquiring look his way. "Sometimes I'm not so sure."

"What do you mean?"

"You tell me. Every time I mention her name, you look away. Obviously something is going on that she's told Brenda, who told you. I sure wish somebody would let me in on the secret."

Richard looked into the depths of his beer.

"Maggie isn't sick or anything, is she?" I asked with sudden worry.

"Oh, no," he quickly reassured me.

"Then what's going on?"

"I've been sworn to secrecy," Richard said gravely.

"Do I have anything to worry about?" I asked, almost afraid to hear his answer.

He shook his head. "Not with Maggie."

I exhaled a mental breath. She had cheated on me before—but for some reason I had faith that would never happen again.

"It's Holly," Richard said.

"Holly?" Maggie's golden retriever. I'd never had a pet until I'd adopted my late father's cat, Herschel, but I'd also come to love Maggie's gentle soul of a dog, too. "What's wrong?"

"Maggie was going to tell you on Saturday, until you told her about our trip. She found a lump on Holly's back on Thursday. The dog was scheduled for surgery this morning."

"Oh, man. My poor Maggs must be beside herself."

"She knew how important it was for you to put all this crap behind you. She didn't want to add to your problems."

I shook my head. "That dog means the world to her."

"Yeah. We're pretty fond of her, too," Richard said. Holly had stayed with Richard and Brenda for a week the year before when someone was stalking Brenda. Only it was me she'd saved when a guy came at me with a knife.

"The thing is, it could be nothing. When quizzed, she told me the mass moved. I'm pretty sure it's just a cyst, but Maggie's terrified she's going to lose her girl."

"Did you tell her what you think?"

"Yeah, but in this case, I'm just a doctor—not a vet—so I'm not sure my opinion counts."

"Will Holly have to stay at the vet overnight?"

He shook his head. "She should be home tonight. But Maggie won't get the pathology report until at least Wednesday. Do you think we'll be going home by then?"

"I don't know. It depends on what I learn tomorrow."

"What *did* you learn today?" he asked, taking another sip of his beer.

"I don't connect with Detective Baldwin, but I get the feeling he knows who killed Shelley but doesn't have enough evidence to move forward."

"That video we saw was certainly inconclusive,"

Richard commented. "So how did you know the guy was Russian?"

I explained, and he nodded.

"The Russian mafia had a substantial presence here in the city back in the nineteen nineties, but they're pretty much history these days."

"So the guy who killed Shelley was some kind of rogue?" Richard asked.

"Rogue, yes. But not just some nobody."

"And that means?" Richard asked.

"I have no idea. I hope I'll have a better understanding tomorrow."

"What if you don't?"

"I don't know. But there's one thing I'm sure of. I can't go back home by plane."

"I kind of figured that," Richard said and polished off the last of his beer. "That leaves going home by train or car. I don't know about you, but I'm not up for a nine- or ten-hour drive."

"It could take even longer by train. And the thing is, you don't have to babysit me. I could take a Greyhound back to Buffalo."

"And arrive a week later? I don't think so."

"It's not that bad."

"And you know because you've done it so many times?" he asked.

I shook my head. I'd also never taken a train trip. Used the subway? Yeah. Hundreds—if not thousands—of times before, but I'd never been on a passenger train.

"I've never been on a train," Richard admitted, too.

So, we were even on that count.

"It might be kind of fun," he said.

"Ya think?" I asked. "Aren't you in a hurry to get back to Brenda and Betsy?"

"Yeah, but before I ever knew Brenda—before we even thought we'd have a child—I had you."

I shook my head at the irony of his comment. "Not anything you ever wanted or expected."

"No, but there you were. And I did a piss-poor job of being your guardian."

No way did I want to get into *that* discussion.

"So, I'm thinking that a train ride home might be kind of fun."

"Rich," I said, deadly serious, "have you *ever* had fun in your entire life?"

"Well … no," he admitted. "But I'm willing to try."

Again, I shook my head. "Me, too. And thanks."

Richard nodded. "So, do we have lunch here, or do we go somewhere else?"

I looked around the room at the clientele. They weren't hostile, and we hadn't been dissed, but we weren't exactly kindred spirits, either. "We can go somewhere else. Coming back here lets me put certain things to rest. I feel good about that."

"Good. Have you got another place you want to visit?"

I shook my head. "I'm pretty much done with Manhattan. Except for what we might learn tomorrow or Wednesday, I'm good to go back home to Buffalo."

"Home?" Richard asked.

"Yeah. It's my home. That's where you, and Brenda, and Betsy, and Maggie are. And it's a pretty nice place." I thought better of it. "Except for winter. That still sucks."

"It sure does. Maybe next year we can go south for a few weeks."

"I wish. Maggie's got a job—and come to think of it, so do I. But until Betsy goes to school, you could get away from winter for a few months."

"And leave you? I don't think so."

"You may one day eat your words," I told him, quoting what he'd told me on an earlier occasion.

"We'll see," he said.

I left a generous tip on the bar and we got up and headed for the exit.

"Thanks for visiting," Maggie the bartender called.

We gave her a wave and headed out the door.

"What are you in the mood for?" Richard asked.

"Nothing exotic."

"Then we could probably duck into any place with a menu that strikes our fancy."

"And then we'd somehow find our way to Tiffany's?"

My brother looked sheepish. "Only if it's convenient. You don't have to come if you don't want to."

I didn't, but only because I knew I could never afford to buy baubles for Maggie there. "Why not? I've never been there before."

Richard said nothing. Obviously he *had* been there.

We continued to walk and stopped at a couple of restaurants until we hit a place that pleased Richard. He wanted steak. I'd be happy with just a burger. The place served both.

The rest of the day yawned before us.

"What do you want to do next?" Richard asked me once we'd finished eating and he'd paid the check.

"I didn't see a chessboard back at the apartment," I said as we started walking back to our home-away-from-home.

"We could get one."

"Why don't we?" I said.

He smiled. "And how about dinner?"

"If you don't mind, I'd rather get take-out and eat in."

"We could do that. Or maybe hit a grocery store."

"Either or. It makes no difference to me."

Here we were in a city of millions. In a city with tons of things to see and do, and we were content just to spend a few hours of quality time together.

I don't know when I'd felt more content.

We never made it to a toy store. Baldwin called me after six that evening, asking us to meet him at Riker's Island the next morning at ten. An inmate, named Gary King, was supposed to know about the guy who killed Shelley.

Richard spent nearly an hour on a face-to-face chat with Brenda, while I called Maggie. I played dumb about her dog and she didn't mention it, but I could tell by the timber of her voice that she was upset and felt like a heel for not pressing her on it. But that was the way she wanted it, and I didn't want to rat out Richard for saying anything.

Richard booked a cab and we arrived at the prison the next morning at 9:55.

Baldwin was waiting. He led us through the security checkpoint and then to yet another interrogation room.

"Have you talked to the guy?" I asked as I sat down behind yet another steel-and-Formica table.

"Yeah."

"So you know what he's got to say?"

"Essentially," Baldwin admitted.

I shifted my gaze to Richard, who shrugged.

We waited. And waited. And waited some more. We'd been there more than twenty minutes, with not much to say to one another, before a black inmate, probably in his late thirties, in an orange jumpsuit, his hands shackled at his waist, was brought into the room.

Baldwin made the introductions. "Shelley Resnick— the woman killed in Grand Central—was Mr. Resnick's wife."

"Sorry for your loss," King muttered, not meeting my gaze.

His condolences were unexpected.

"Thanks," I said, and meant it.

"So," Baldwin began, his gaze fixed on King. "You said you knew about the murder."

"She was one of my girls," King said.

Her pimp? Goddamn. My beautiful Shelley had acquired a stinking pimp? He probably cashed in on her—lived off her and God knows how many others. But weren't pimps supposed to keep their girls safe? Unless maybe she'd ripped him off, too.

"So you set her up with a john and then she was killed," Baldwin said.

"Fucking nasty Russian. I took care of my girls—but that fucker was crazy. I didn't know that when I set things up the first time."

"So, you're saying that when Shelley was killed you had nothing to do with her meeting with the Russian that night?" I asked.

"Hell, no. But that bitch—" King stopped abruptly, and looked at me in horror. "Sorry, man."

"It's okay," I assured him. "Go on."

"She done told one of my other girls that the Russian liked her. He was gonna give her some fine shit. She gave him her cell phone number and told him he could save a hundred bucks if he called her direct."

"She screwed you, too," I said without rancor.

"I may be a pimp, but I protect my girls," King said adamantly. "I can't do that when they go off on their own."

I almost laughed, and yet I got the sense the guy was being honest with me.

"Come on, Gary," Baldwin said. "You controlled your girls by giving them only enough drugs to do your bidding."

King's eyes blazed. "I gave them a safe place to live. They had food on the table, cable TV, and they only had to turn a couple of tricks a day. I had me a high-class operation. My mistake was taking on that white girl. I felt sorry for her. She was in way over her head, but she was a nice little girl. She needed somebody to protect her."

He turned to glare at me.

"Hey, man, I bailed her out time and again, tried to help her get clean. She left *me*. She didn't *want* me. She didn't want *my* help."

King shrugged. "Yeah. She kinda told me so."

"What about this Russian guy?" Richard asked. "Did you get his name? Anything on him?"

"I saw his car. A black Lexus with diplomat plates."

I looked over at Baldwin. He'd heard this story before.

"And?" I pressed.

"And nothing. That's all I know."

"No name?"

King shook his head.

"What did he look like?"

"Mean. He wasn't old, but he had a full head of silver hair. That's all I remember."

"Which is jack shit," Baldwin said.

"How many silver-haired, commie diplomats driving a black Lexus can there be in this city?" King asked.

"That was four years ago—forever," Baldwin barked. "That guy could have returned to Moscow the day after the murder.

King's eyes narrowed. "I'm telling you what I know. You just don't give a shit. You don't care about that girl." Again he turned to glare at me. "I did when nobody else would."

"Thanks, man. I'm glad someone was looking out for Shelley," I said.

Again King shrugged. He looked at Baldwin. "Are we done?"

"Yeah." Baldwin nodded to the two guards who had stayed planted just inside the interrogation room's door. King got up from his chair, and the guards moved to flank him. "You'll get that bastard—if you want to," he told Baldwin, and then exited the room.

I listened as the three sets of footsteps on the concrete

floor echoed and then faded before I turned and spoke to Baldwin. "Have you got the name of the guy who killed my wife?"

"Sort of. The problem is ... he's got diplomatic immunity."

Oh, yeah. I knew about that. Diplomats—and the members of their staffs—had some of the worst reputations, and a lot of them committed petty crimes on a regular basis just because they could. The most common being parking infractions. I hadn't owned a car while living in Manhattan because the cost of parking was more than a month's rent—which wasn't cheap even for the hovels I'd lived in. Anyone with diplomat plates parked wherever the hell they pleased at any time of the day or night because they knew there'd be no consequences—unlike the rest of us, who'd be towed in a heartbeat. And even if they committed murder, it wasn't likely to land them in the pokey because—Geeze Louise—what if one of our guys did the same thing while in their country? So, diplomats moved around the city with impunity.

"You're not going to tell me the name of the man who killed my wife, are you?" I asked Baldwin.

"You said you were psychic. Aren't you supposed to tell *me* how things went down?"

"Not really."

"My brother has empathic abilities," Richard explained. The fact that he had an MD after his name gave him more credibility than if I'd uttered the same phrase. At least to some.

"I would have to encounter the bastard, get him to think about killing Shelley—and probably touch him—before I could get anything on him. I depend on a tactile interface to get stuff on people—if I can even connect with them," I told Baldwin.

"Well, that's not likely to happen."

"Is the guy still in town?" I asked.

Baldwin nodded. "We suspect he's killed at least another four prostitutes since your wife's death, but we haven't got enough to pin him down."

"Can't you at least deport the scumbag?"

"So he can just kill prostitutes in his homeland?" Baldwin shrugged. Did he figure a whore was a whore and it didn't matter that her executioner was likely to keep killing no matter where he landed?

"It looks like we made the trip from Buffalo for nothing," Richard said with bitterness.

Baldwin nodded toward me. "*He* said he might get some insight from touching the evidence."

It was unfortunate that what I got was no more than what the detective already knew, and I said so. There was no point in asking him for more details on the Russian; I knew he wasn't going to share them.

"So, I guess you're ready to go home," Baldwin said.

"Maybe. Maybe not. I've been away for two years. There are people and places I'd like to reconnect with."

Richard turned to look at me, his expression grim. He was more than ready to return to his wife and daughter. I wasn't.

Baldwin's gaze was still riveted on me. "I talked to your former bosses. You were a trained investigator and you were good. Damn good, they said."

Oh, yeah? Too bad that hadn't saved my friggin' job.

"So what are you saying?" I asked, playing dumb.

"Don't go looking for the Russian."

"You've given me nothing to go on."

"No, but if your insight is even half as good as your investigative skills, you might be able to track the guy down."

"And even if I could, what do you expect me to do? Kill the bastard?"

"That's not beyond the realm of possibility."

I offered the detective a wan smile. "But you forget;

I've made a whole new life. I've got a family back in Buffalo. I've got a lady there, too. Why would I blow all that for a woman who left me, who bled me dry?"

"Because you loved the bitch," Baldwin said bluntly.

I looked away, stung. Was he right? Was I stupid enough to sacrifice what I had—and my future—to avenge Shelley's death?

I wasn't sure.

We took a cab back to Manhattan and somehow ended up at Tiffany's. I followed Richard and looked at case after case of amazing jewelry and felt like a piece of shit because there wasn't one sparkling item I could afford to buy for my sweet Maggie. Richard bought a pair of gold-and-diamond earrings for Brenda and they were placed in that distinctive little blue box. I'd spent my excess cash on a decent coat for the trip and had nothing to spare for a gift for Maggie.

Next up was a trip to Toys "R" Us. Richard heeded my suggestion and didn't buy a six-foot stuffed polar bear for his baby girl, but he didn't go on the cheap for a chess board, either. He picked out a set made of white marble and black granite, which weighed a ton, and made arrangements to have it delivered to the apartment. By then, it was lunchtime and we settled on an elegant restaurant not far from the apartment.

We ordered drinks before Richard's expression turned grim as he faced me. "Now what do we do?"

"You can go home if you want. I want to stay for a few days."

"To track down the Russian?"

I answered honestly. "Yes."

"And then what?"

"I don't know."

"Where would you start?"

"A few years back, I'd contact a buddy of mine at the DMV. The problem is, since I got whacked on the head by those muggers, I can't even remember the guy's name."

"Other than roaming the streets of the city, where else would you go?"

"I might visit the UN."

"I've never been there, "Richard admitted.

"Neither have I."

"What do you think you might find there?"

I shrugged. "I don't know. It might be nice to take a tour. I'm sure they give them."

"A few years back, Brenda and I went to Asheville to see Biltmore. They gave private tours that went behind the scenes and let us see and touch stuff the regular tourists weren't privy to."

"Do you think the UN does that, too?"

"They might. If one paid enough."

"That lets me out."

"But not me—and a guest."

"What are you thinking?" I asked, staring into his intense blue eyes.

"That on a private tour one could actually sit in the seats of the Russian delegation."

"And if I got nothing?"

"You'd learn some nice history about US-Russian relationships since the League of Nations was supplanted by the UN."

I gave him a wry smile. "I do like to think of myself as a bit of a history buff. In fourteen-hundred and ninety-two, Columbus sailed the ocean blue."

"That, too," Richard said with amusement.

We were on the same page.

"I'm not sure I'm up to it today—or even if we could schedule it this late in the afternoon."

"I'll do some research when we get back to the apartment. I presume you'll need to crash for a few hours."

"No, not really." Two years after the mugging, I was beginning to make real progress on that front.

Richard smiled. "Good. So, should we find a grocery store or order in for supper?"

"You're no cook."

"And you're not much better."

"So maybe we should order a pizza instead."

"We could."

"Sounds like a plan."

"What about breakfast tomorrow?"

"We could hit the same deli I went to yesterday. I assume you wouldn't want more for breakfast."

"Not really."

"Then let's do that. Then after that, I need a little FaceTime with Brenda and Betsy."

"Oh, the wonders of the world-wide net."

"Will you call Maggie tonight?"

"I don't think I want to talk about what we learned today—and I know she'll ask."

Richard nodded. "I can tell Brenda what went down and ask her to share it with Maggie."

I thought about it for a moment. "That's probably a good idea. If you'll loan me your iPad, I'll email Maggie a quick note."

Again he nodded.

We kept walking and in less than five minutes had arrived at our temporary digs. The concierge announced that our chess board had been delivered and awaited us upstairs.

Once back in the apartment, I went to my room to change into my real-life clothes, while Richard called his friends in California. Within an hour, his former secretary and friend had arranged a private tour of the UN for us for the next day. Then Richard changed into what he considered his grungies—Dockers and a cashmere sweater—and we set up the chess board. We played a couple of games before ordering a loaded pizza.

Later, after we'd messaged our loved ones, we watched college basketball on the tube. March madness was about to start. We took opposite teams and cheered and swore and tried not to think about what we'd learned about Shelley's death during the past thirty-six hours.

But that night all the horror came back to assault my psyche in the form of nightmares. Four years out, I knew it would take a long, long time for me to come to terms with Shelley's gruesome death.

The next morning we killed time by reading the paper with our coffee and bagels and then we took a walk around the neighborhood. Richard seemed restless; he strode forward with his hands thrust into the pockets of his heavy winter coat, and in no mood to chat. I wasn't feeling that talkative, either. I had too much on my mind.

Back at the apartment, we changed back into business attire, then took a cab to the UN's General Assembly Building and checked in with the information desk. We were met by a petite Asian woman.

"Dr. Alpert?"

"That's me," Richard said. "And this is my brother, Jeff Resnick."

She nodded. "I'm Lisa Chang." Her English was perfect. "I'll be your guide this morning."

"Thank you."

"I understand you gentlemen are from Buffalo."

"That we are," Richard said.

"I'm from Batavia."

"Get out," I said, and actually smiled.

"I swear," Lisa said. "I went to school at UB."

Richard's smile widened. "So did I."

"It's a small world," Lisa said. "It will be my pleasure to show a couple of my homies around the UN."

Lisa launched into a well-rehearsed speech about the history of the place, the architecture, and led us around the building. It was all very interesting, but I found myself looking at every guy in the place, searching for a silver-haired man who resembled Vladimir Putin—not that I even had a clue what Shelley's killer actually looked like.

Richard and Lisa chatted away. He asked loads of questions and she happily answered them, but I couldn't seem to concentrate on a word they exchanged.

It wasn't until she led us into the General Assembly Hall that I was able to absorb the gist of what she was saying. I looked around the cavernous room clad in rich wood paneling, with two Jumbotrons flanking either side of the magnificent granite podium. The carpet between the delegates' seats was green, the chairs a buff-colored leather, and black rectangular signs with glowing blue lettering marked the delegates' assigned seating. There were a lot of them. How the hell was I going to find where the Russians sat during open sessions?

Richard was my savior. "Can we go up to the podium and look out at the whole room?"

"No problem," Lisa said cheerfully. She seemed keen to please a fellow alumnus.

We followed her down the aisle and mounted the area around the podium, looking out at the hundreds of seats we'd so often seen on TV or in the print news media.

"Where does the US delegation sit?" Richard asked.

Lisa pointed. "Over there."

"And Canada?"

"Over there."

"How about the Russian delegation?"

I watched as Lisa's arm swung around to point again.

Richard knew what I needed to do, so he moved to stand off to one side, and Lisa instantly turned to face him. He kept her engaged in conversation, giving me the opportunity to slip away. I practically jogged up the sloping aisle, making my way over the block of five seats.

I knew I didn't have much time and sat down in the first chair, settling my arms on the rests, my fingers grasping the material, hoping to gain some kind of knowledge, or glom onto some dark feelings. Unfortunately, I got nothing. Nada. Zilch.

I moved over one chair and something inside me thrummed. The man who regularly sat here felt strongly about something. I shut my eyes and concentrated, trying to home in on the emotion that permeated the fabric. Slowly I managed to interpret the strong feeling ... homesickness. As marvelous as New York was, it wasn't home, and the man who regularly sat there was counting the days until his assignment was over and he could return to Mother Russia. *Hope you get to go home soon, buddy.* I moved to the next seat.

No sooner had my ass hit the chair than I knew I'd hit pay dirt. I'm not exactly sure what it was I was feeling, just a sense of malevolence. Whoever sat there on a regular basis felt contempt for Americans—and American women in particular. He saw them as objects—for his pleasure and as sport.

I shuddered in revulsion, but I didn't get up. I needed to glom onto as much of this bastard as I could—try to experience who he was—what kind of sadistic monster he was.

I kept swallowing, afraid I might gag. Soon, my head began to pound. I had to get out of there. I'd gotten what I needed as a start, but I had to have more. A lot more. Could I impose on Richard's former colleagues to cut through red tape and get me the information that would help me track down Shelley's killer?

I stood, still swallowing way too hard. Good God I did not want to embarrass my brother by puking in the UN's General Assembly Hall. I started off toward the exit where I was sure I'd seen a men's room not far from the big doors. I made it to one of the stalls before I tossed my bagel and coffee breakfast and was hit with the dry heaves. Spent, I sat down on the toilet seat, head bowed, elbows on knees with the heels of my palms pressed against my eye sockets until I could think again. Other tourists came to use the facilities and then left. I wasn't sure it would be safe for a cab to have me as a passenger, but maybe once I got outside, the fresh air might help.

Ten minutes after my retreat from the hall, the door to the john opened once again and a familiar voice called, "Jeff?"

"Here."

Soon a pair of polished black shoes appeared just within sight of the closed stall door. "Are you okay?"

"Not really," I answered.

"Is our tour over?" he asked, sounding worried.

"Oh, yeah."

Grasping the toilet paper holder, I hauled myself onto unsteady feet and opened the door. Richard stood before me, looking worried.

"Did you get what you need?"

"Partially."

"What does that mean?"

"It means I need more information." I stared into his worried eyes and waited. He knew his friends in California could give me the information I wanted—*needed*—in only minutes, but he wasn't willing to ask them for it because he feared about how I'd use it.

At that moment, so did I.

I was feeling a lot better by the time we'd walked halfway back to that beautiful apartment. We stopped at a convenience store and Richard bought me a carton of yogurt. He made me eat it right there on the street and I have to admit that, aside from a bit of a headache, I felt a lot better afterward.

"You're a good doctor," I told him as I tossed the plastic container and spoon into a trash can.

He shrugged. "Sometimes."

We started off again.

"What do you want to do next?"

"Gary King described the guy who killed Shelley. He's part of the Russian delegation to the UN. He shouldn't be too hard to find."

"And what would you do if you found him?" Richard asked.

Did I detect fear in his voice?

"I want to meet him."

"And do what?" he persisted.

"I don't know."

"Baldwin is worried that if you knew who the guy was, you'd do something stupid. So am I." We kept walking. "Am I right?"

"I don't know."

Richard grabbed my arm and pulled me out of the pedestrian traffic. "I need your word that you won't do something stupid like go after the guy."

"Rich, I don't own a gun and I'm half the size of the goon who killed Shelley. What could I do to bring the bastard down?"

"You're nothing if not resourceful."

"I take that as a compliment."

"But you still can't promise you won't try to get back at him."

I hesitated before answering. "I don't know."

"That's not good enough."

"That's the best I can do."

He looked at me, his eyes welling with tears.

"Rich, have I ever really disappointed you?"

He swallowed. "No."

"Then I promise you, I won't disappoint you now."

He nodded. "Okay. That's good enough for me."

I felt like hugging him, but that was his style—not mine. So I gave him what I hoped was an encouraging smile. He nodded, but wasn't able to reciprocate. We started off again.

"I feel a lot better since I ate that yogurt."

"The enzymes help promote digestive harmony," he said, distracted.

"My gut is definitely singing a happier song."

"Are you up to having lunch?"

"Maybe in another half an hour or so."

"Good. Shall we keep walking?"

"I'd like to. When I lived here, I walked everywhere. That's not conducive back in Buffalo."

"Brenda's looking forward to spring when we can take Betsy for walks around the neighborhood in her stroller."

"That'll be nice. I may even take her out myself—Maggie and I," I amended. I needed him to believe I had plans for the future—plans beyond the next day or so.

"I'm sure she'll love it."

We didn't talk much during the next half hour. We consulted a number of menus before Richard chose a restaurant. We were shown to a table by the window and ordered a couple of beers, which arrived in record time, and then Richard consulted his iPhone while I stared, unseeing, at the menu in my hands. Already a plan was beginning to formulate in my mind. As King had said, how many Russian diplomats with silver hair and a Lexus could there be in the city? But I was also worried that Baldwin might assign someone to follow us. That probably wouldn't happen for at least another day—if ever—but I didn't want to take that chance.

Richard finally set his phone down and picked up his menu. "What looks good to you?"

"I don't know. A ham sandwich, I guess."

"You've been thinking," he accused.

"I think all day—every day."

"About Shelley's killer?"

"Just a little," I admitted.

"What are you going to do about him?"

"I don't know."

"You're a law-abiding citizen," Richard said adamantly, as though saying it with enough conviction would insure it.

"For the most part."

"I don't like the sound of that."

"I admit it. Sometimes I do more than thirty-five miles per hour while driving down Main Street. Do you think that warrants jail time?"

"That's not what I'm talking about."

"Then just what *are* you talking about?"

"Your soul."

I couldn't help but laugh. "You know I don't believe in that shit."

"Oh, no? What about Sophie? What about my grand-mother?"

"Earth-bound spirits. Even they couldn't explain what's beyond our five senses."

The waitress arrived. "Ready to order?" she asked hopefully.

"We'll have another round," Richard said. "And I'll have a Reuben."

"I'll have a ham and Swiss cheese sandwich on rye bread."

"We don't have that on our menu," the waitress said.

"Do you have ham in any capacity?" I asked.

"Yes," she answered uncertainly. "But we don't do ham sandwiches."

"But that's absurd."

She shrugged. "Sorry."

"This is a restaurant. They serve sandwiches," I in-sisted.

"Jeff," Richard admonished.

And suddenly I was as angry as Jack Nicholson in *Five Easy Pieces* when he couldn't get a couple of lousy pieces of toast. "Then I'm sure the chef can come up with ham on bread with a slice of cheese, and if not, then I can walk out the door to find it elsewhere."

"It's your choice," the waitress said. She'd obviously never heard the old saw that the customer was always right.

I leveled an angry glare at my beloved brother, who wasn't comfortable with any kind of conflict. "I'm done," I said with as much calm as I could muster, and stood. "I'll see you back at the apartment."

"Jeff, wait!" Richard called, but I pivoted and headed out of the restaurant.

I didn't know where I would go or what I would do, but I knew I needed some alone time. If I high-tailed it quick enough, Richard would have to settle the bar tab and be unable to catch up with me. He'd be pissed, but I couldn't help that.

The chilled air hit me like a smack in the face and I turned right, away from our home-away-from home. I needed to walk a couple of miles on mindless autopilot because I wasn't sure what I felt and what I needed to do with the information I'd learned that day.

I needed to get online, but the days of cyber cafes were long gone. I supposed I could use my phone, but texting really isn't my thing—my thumbs go numb. The apartment building had a shared office center with a couple of computers, printers, and a fax machine, but I needed a little anonymity. There was only one other place I could think of to go.

I ducked into the first store I came to, pulled out my phone and Googled the location of the nearest library. Next, I turned off the phone. I didn't want Richard hounding me—and I sure as hell didn't want him coming after me, either.

I knew what I needed to do to find the bastard who had killed Shelley. I just wasn't sure what I would do when I tracked him down.

I had to wait more than an hour before one of the computer carrels opened up at the Mid-Manhattan Library, and was thankful they'd provided a big squirt bottle of hand sanitizer for patrons to use. The keyboard was incredibly cruddy, but I had more on my mind than the number and kinds of bacteria that inhabited it.

I no longer had access to the data bases I regularly perused when I was just another minion in the vast insurance industry, but I also knew the kinds of keywords that would get me places and access to data that the average man on the street couldn't retrieve. It took me less than an hour to identify every member of the Russian diplomatic staff. The head guy was Alexey Bykov. It wasn't all that hard to get his picture and home address, and that of all his staff, too. If I were one of them, I'd be nervous about how easy it was to track them down but, hey, I wasn't about to complain and made plans to better cover my own Internet tracks once I was back home in Buffalo.

See, I did *not* have a death wish.

Honest.

But I also wasn't sure I didn't harbor particularly vicious murderous thoughts, either.

Only one member of Bykov's staff had silver hair. He kind of reminded me of what Maggie called Blond Bond, the actor, Daniel Craig. Unfortunately, in this scenario, Sergei Kovshutin was playing villain—not good guy.

I logged off the computer and wondered what to do next. It was damn cold outside, but maybe the layers that had me sweating for the past hour would be good enough to thwart the March temps outside. I didn't want to go back to the apartment to change because then I'd have to explain things to Richard and that was not on my list of things to do.

I logged off, got up from the uncomfortable office chair, strode straight out the building and turned left. The wind had died, so the air didn't seem as chilly as it had earlier in the day. Still, it was going to be quite a hike, but I wasn't about to take a cab to old Sergei's apartment. No way did I want anyone to be able to testify that I'd ever been there.

It was going on six o'clock when I stood across the street from the twenty-story glass-fronted building. I had no idea how long I was going to have to stay wedged at the head of an alley that served a deli and a dry cleaner. It didn't matter. I had hours and hours to kill.

Hands shoved into my pockets, I stamped my feet on the concrete to keep warm. Why hadn't I thought to wear a hat and gloves before leaving the damn apartment that morning?

It was almost dark when the silver-haired Russian, wearing shades on that dull gray evening, strode down the sidewalk on the opposite side of the street and entered the luxury apartment building. Sergei's apartment was on the sixteenth floor, way higher than I was ever willing to live. In a fire, the NYFD's cherry-picker trucks could reach the seventh floor to effect a rescue, and those above had a nasty choice to make: jump, or risk death from smoke inhalation from the long walk down a soot-filled stairwell. I was glad I lived above Richard's garage. If push came to shove, I could break a window and dangle with only a five or six foot drop.

I stood rooted on the hard concrete, occasionally stamping my feet to keep the circulation going. I didn't do much thinking, too preoccupied with waiting for Sergei. I did not want to miss him. I still had no plan other than to wait and watch.

Time dragged as night closed in.

One hour ....

Two hours ....

My feet were popsicles and I wondered how much longer I could stand the cold when Sergei emerged through the big glass doors of his apartment building. Although the sun had set long ago, the jerk still wore sunglasses. Who did he think he was? Bono? He headed north, and I took off as well, shadowing him from the other side of the street.

The guy oozed confidence. Why not? He'd probably already killed five women with impunity. Did he think of himself as a twenty-first century Jack-the-Ripper? Okay, he didn't eviscerate his victims, but when he was finished with them, they were just as dead.

I followed him as he zig-and-zagged down the streets of Manhattan. I kept far enough back so that he had no idea he was being followed. The guy walked with such an exaggerated swagger that I could almost hear the Bee Gees singing *Stayin' Alive* in the back of my mind. Finally, he ducked into a bar called Henry's. I waited a full minute before I casually entered the establishment.

The place was welcoming, with its dark-paneled oak, black-painted tin ceiling, and plenty of tables for the dinner crowd, which had already thinned. It was then I remembered that I hadn't had anything to eat but a cup of yogurt since the breakfast I'd upchucked, and the no-ham sandwich policy at the joint Richard had chosen for lunch. Only a couple of TVs with closed-captioning spoiled the bar's otherwise vintage charm.

Sergei had already scored a stool and had taken off his shades, which sat on the bar. He'd apparently arrived there on a mission, and was already conversing with a black woman who was dressed to the nines. Was she a prostitute? If so, she was high-end. She had a pretty smile, and for some reason I got the feeling she was nobody's fool. But I also wondered if she'd be Sergei's next victim.

I took a seat four stools down from the Russian and pretended I was looking at one of the TV screens, keeping him at the edge of my peripheral vision. He pulled out his smartphone and was swiping the screen, oblivious to what was going on around him. My gut tightened and I had to swallow down revulsion. This joker was alive and breathing. Shelley was dead and buried.

I hadn't been inside the bar for more than thirty seconds when someone sat down beside me.

Richard.

"What the hell are you doing here?" he muttered, just loud enough for me to hear.

"More important; what the hell are *you* doing here?"

"I'm thirsty."

"Bullshit."

I realized what his appearance meant. "You followed me?"

"Someone has to keep you from doing something incredibly stupid."

"And what would that be?"

He lowered his voice. "Committing murder."

I turned to glare at him. "Why in *hell* would you think that?"

"You like the world to think you have no emotions, but you're just the opposite. You feel things far more intensely than the rest of us."

I was about to refute that statement when the bartender spoke up.

"What can I get you gents?" the lady asked. She was pretty. Blue eyes, auburn hair—not unlike my dear sweet Maggie—only twenty years younger.

"Heineken," I said, struggling to keep my voice calm.

"Me, too," Richard said.

"Bottles only," she said.

"Not a problem," Richard replied.

Once the bartender turned away, Richard leaned forward to look around me, taking in the Russian. "So, what are you planning?"

I stared at the reflection of Shelley's murderer's face in the mirror behind the bar. "Nothing. I'm just here to observe."

"What? His drinking habits?"

It looked like the Russian had ordered a Scotch on the rocks; his companion had nothing. Was he too stingy to buy her one, or was she determined to keep a clear head?

I should have taken a seat closer to the guy, then I could have listened in on their conversation, not that he was paying all that much attention to the woman, who had picked up his sunglasses and was idly toying with them.

Our beers arrived, along with a couple of napkins and glasses, and Richard paid the tab. He poured his, but I was too busy watching the Russian to pour mine.

"What are you going to do when you leave here?"

"I have no idea," I said truthfully. I wasn't sure what I was feeling besides the most obvious: anger. I wanted to throttle the guy. He was the reason my wife was dead. But if I was honest with myself, Shelley's dangerous behavior would have gotten her killed sooner or later—the Russian had just been the first to see her as easy prey and had taken advantage of her gullibility. Shelley thought she'd become street smart, but she hadn't wised up soon enough.

"What a waste," I muttered, and finally grabbed the bottle, pouring the beer so it left virtually no head.

"Shelley? Or the silver fox?" Richard asked quietly, and took a sip of his beer.

"Both. Her life—and him being a waste of space."

The waste of space pocketed his phone and finally started paying attention to his Scotch.

I kept my attention riveted on the mirror. "I turned

off my phone. How were you able to track me?"

"I know how to get around certain protocols." I knew he wasn't bragging.

I picked up my glass, and noticed my hand was shaking. I took a sip of beer, but was afraid I'd slop it all over the bar and set it back down again. What the hell was I going to do? I could follow Sergei for the rest of the evening. I could tail him for weeks. I could buy a gun off the street and blast a hole through the back of his skull like he'd done to Shelley.

I could.

But I knew I wouldn't.

The truth is I'm a coward. I like my life. It was getting better all the time. Doing time in jail for the next quarter century was not on my agenda. And yet ... someone needed to take this guy out. Someone *needed* to make him pay for the suffering he'd caused not just me, but the families of the other women he'd murdered.

Someone. But not me.

And for some reason, I felt ashamed. Ashamed I didn't have the balls to take on the contemptible prick. Ashamed that I wasn't up to avenging Shelley's murder.

I turned to my brother. "We'd better go home."

"When?"

"Tonight."

He scrutinized my face, his own mirroring his obvious relief. "You mean it?"

I nodded. "Yeah."

He let out a shaky breath. "Thank God."

God had nothing to do with it.

"I don't think we can hop a train back to Buffalo at this time of night."

"Then we'll rent a car. I know you said you didn't want to drive, but—"

"Who says we have to drive straight through?" he asked. "I've never been to Cooperstown. It might be fun to stop and take a look around."

"I didn't know you were that into baseball."

"Brenda and I take in at least one Bisons game a year. And there's the Farmer's Museum there, too."

He didn't give a damn about visiting museums. He just wanted to get me out of the city before I could do something stupid—and I was going to let him.

"I guess it wouldn't hurt to look at a scythe, some plows, and maybe an old wagon or two." I tried to laugh, but couldn't. I felt heartsick.

Sergei pushed back his stool and stood. He spoke into his companion's ear, and then headed toward the back of the bar—for the can, no doubt.

The woman got up and headed for the door.

The Russian had left his sunglasses on the bar.

I looked around. No one was paying attention to me. I quickly stood, took two steps forward, and grabbed them by the earpiece, clasping it so hard my knuckles whitened.

"Jeff!" Richard sounded angry.

I moved back to my seat, kept my hand close to my body so that no one—not even Richard—could see what I held. My breaths came faster as I tried to make sense of the feelings and emotions that clung to the plastic in my clenched fist. It wasn't getting anything on the Russian— it was the vibes his companion had left that assaulted my psyche.

A smoldering anger topped the list. She'd done a good job hiding it. In fact, I would have sworn she'd looked bored during the minutes she'd sat beside Sergei. And the anger was much deeper than that of a woman being ig- nored in a bar. Hateful anger. Anger I could identify with. Anger because of what Sergei had done to her—or hers, but I had no clue what it was. I could, however, specu- late.

She had a plan.

She had a switchblade that was nestled against a packet of tissues and a wad of cash in the beaded clutch that had rested on her lap the entire time she'd sat at the bar. The knife was a thing of beauty, with a pink pearl-like handle and a polished chrome blade. Exquisite—and deadly.

And she intended to use it.

The Russian returned from the john, bypassing the bar and heading for the exit. He held the door open for his companion, and they exited the bar. I watched them stand in front of the door's beveled glass. He patted down his coat, looking for something. He spoke to her, and she nodded. She opened the door and came back inside, heading straight for the seats they'd so recently vacated.

She glanced around the bar, then under the chairs.

"Did you lose something?" I asked.

"Yes. A pair of sunglasses."

"I found these on the bar. I was going to turn them into the bartender," I lied. She moved closer and I handed them to her.

"Thank you."

She was about to turn, when I caught the sleeve of her coat. I pulled her close and whispered in her ear. I could feel her immediately tense as she listened to what I had to tell her. Then she turned and glared at me. She said nothing. She didn't have to.

She yanked her arm from my grasp, straightened, and once again left the bar.

I didn't watch her leave. Instead, I turned back to my beer.

"What did you tell her?" Richard asked.

"Not now," I told him. "Later." But that wasn't exactly a promise. I drained my beer. "We need to get the hell out of the city—and as soon as possible."

"I don't like the sound of this."

"Let's grab a cab, pack our stuff, go to the airport, rent

a car, and start for home ASAP."

"Now you're scaring the shit out of me."

I thought about it. It might be better to first stop in a few convenience stores to better establish an alibi—because I was going to need one. Mr. Kovshutin was likely to meet his maker in the next few hours and I wanted to make sure that there was no way I could be implicated for what might be his rather grisly death.

Gosh-darn-it, somehow I couldn't work up a whole helluva lot of sympathy for the guy.

I stood. "Let's go. The sooner we head for home, the sooner we can kiss my little Cherry Pie." My pet name for Richard's sweet baby girl.

"I'm all for that," he agreed.

In many ways, Richard is a lot more worldly than me, but after living fourteen years in the city, I could still grab a cab a helluva lot faster than him.

Within minutes, we were back at our apartment, and ten minutes later, we waited in the lobby for yet another cab to arrive.

We didn't say a word to each other on the way to the White Plains airport, where Richard had already reserved a rental car. We picked up the keys for a bronze Lexus, stowed our luggage, and I took the first shift behind the wheel as we steered for the Tappan Zee Bridge. The car's headlights cut a swath of light on the double-lane road as we headed north toward Albany. I was glad the night sky was clear with no snow in the forecast.

"When are you going to tell me what went down between you and that woman at the bar?" Richard asked. "What did you say to her?"

"Not much," I admitted. "I told her to look out for surveillance cameras."

"What the hell does that mean?" Richard asked. I don't think I'd ever heard such a note of fear in his voice.

"Sadly, Mr. Kovshutin isn't long for this world."

"She's going to kill him?" he asked, aghast.

"I got that feeling."

"Oh, man," he said, sounding heartsick.

"Rich, that guy *killed* my wife. He's *killed* others. At least four other women that the police know about. Who knows how many others he's abused in the interim?"

"Yes, but ... murdering him? I dunno."

"An eye for an eye," I quoted.

"I'm a doctor. I swore an oath to Hippocrates."

"Nobody's asking *you* to terminate a killer."

"Yeah, but you know a murder is going to happen and you aren't going to stop it."

"I don't *know* that a murder is going to happen. I only know that it could be a possibility."

"And you didn't try to stop her," he reiterated. "In fact, you may have helped to *make* it happen."

I said nothing.

"I can't believe you approve of murder," he tried again, disappointment heavy in his tone.

"I approve of justice." Though our contact was brief, I knew the woman in the bar had suffered as devastating a loss as me. She knew Kovshutin was never going to pay for his crimes, so she was determined to deliver her *own* brand of justice.

"Did you consider the alternative?"

"What do you mean?"

"That woman might attempt murder and become that bastard's next victim."

I shook my head. "That wasn't the impression I got. Look, I don't think we should discuss this anymore."

"Why? Because you don't want to acknowledge your guilt?"

"No. Because I don't *feel* any guilt, and that pisses you off."

"I don't know what to say," Richard said, obviously frustrated.

"It's karma, Rich," I said, my gaze riveted on the road ahead of me. "What goes around comes around."

"The *law* should handle these things."

"All well and good for average citizens, but we're talking about a guy with diplomatic immunity."

"And that's just *wrong*," he asserted.

"But you can't change it, and neither can I."

He let out what sounded like a frustrated breath. "I guess you're right."

We drove another mile before I spoke again. "Think of it this way, those women that the scumbag killed might finally find peace."

"And how about you?"

"I haven't had a decent night's sleep since the day Shelley admitted she was into drugs. I'm looking forward to a night of undisturbed slumber."

"Are you sure you can live with what you've done—or, rather, haven't done to stop that man's death?"

I wished I wasn't driving at the time, I would have liked to have looked him in the eye when I answered, "Yes."

We stopped in Utica to top up the gas tank and grab something to eat. Richard resisted the urge to call Brenda to let her know how far we'd traveled. I could tell he was pissed at me by the lack of conversation between us during the previous few hours. He fell asleep before we hit Syracuse and I continued to drive west.

The only scenery in the dead of night was of cars and trucks overtaking us, and the periodic glow of the green highway signs. The Thruway cut across rural New York giving no hint of the skyscrapers (what there were of them) that populated the bigger cities.

It was nearly four in the morning when we approached the Buffalo toll booths. The car slowing roused

Richard from sleep.

"Good morning, Sleeping Beauty."

Richard rubbed bleary eyes. "I was supposed to take over driving hours ago."

"I wasn't tired." I'd had far too much on my mind. Speculation, mostly. None of it pretty or commendable.

Richard fumbled for his wallet, ready to be fleeced by the Thruway Authority. He handed me a ten and the toll ticket. I handed back the change before I steered us toward the Main Street exit.

"You didn't have a chance to call Maggie," Richard said.

"No."

"She has good news."

"About Holly?" I asked.

"The pathology report came back. The dog is going to be okay."

"Good. It'll give me something to celebrate."

"I thought you already had a cause for celebration with the death of Shelley's killer."

I wasn't going to reignite that powder keg of a conversation.

The lights were on in Richard's kitchen when we pulled up his driveway. "Are you going to come in?"

I shook my head. "I've never left Herschel," my cat, "this long. I should go pay some attention to him. Tell Brenda I'll be over later to see her and CP. Then we'll drop off the rental car."

"Right."

We collected our luggage from the trunk of the Lexus and went our separate ways. As anticipated, Herschel was ecstatic to see me—for about a minute. Then he swished his tail and turned, giving me the cold shoulder.

I didn't bother unpacking and grabbed a beer from the fridge, settling on my couch. I didn't bother to turn on the tube and instead wondered if old Sergei had already left this earthly plane. As I'd told Richard, I did not feel guilty. I thought I might feel relief in knowing what had really happened to Shelley, but instead I didn't seem to feel anything at all.

I'd once vowed I'd never visit her grave again, but now I wished we'd taken the time to do it. Right until the end, Shelley had worn the wedding ring I'd slipped on her finger that sunny day in August.

I raised my beer bottle. "Here's to you, Shelley."

Once again the phone rang. I'd known it was going to ring. I'd known who was calling. And again, that didn't make me want to lift the receiver.

"Good morning, Detective Baldwin."

"You got caller ID?" he asked from four hundred miles away.

"No. I always know when you're going to call, only this time I suspect it may be the last time we talk."

"Oh, yeah?"

"You're calling to tell me that Sergei Kovshutin is dead."

"You're right," he said, his voice devoid of inflection.

"And?" I prompted, my lack of emotion mirroring his own.

"He went missing the night you left Manhattan."

"Do tell."

"It seems you had a run-in with him at a bar called Henry's."

"I wouldn't say run-in. I saw him there. My brother and I had a drink and then we left the city."

"Why such an abrupt departure?"

"Because I knew the law wasn't going to do anything to rein him in. What was the point of staying?"

"You haven't asked how he died."

I said nothing.

"The body showed some signs of decomposition, but wasn't in such bad shape that the ME couldn't count the number of stab wounds or see that his throat had been slashed."

"A messy way to go. Do you have any leads?"

"Just that he was seen with a pretty black woman at the bar. Then there was no trace of him until he washed up on the shore of the Hudson River near Jersey City. I was wondering what you knew about it."

"Why would I know anything about it?"

"Because you're *psychic,*" he said with a sneer in his voice.

Again, I said nothing.

"The bar's video shows that you spoke to the woman who was with Kovshutin. What did you tell her?"

"I warned her to be careful."

"And that's all?"

"I was concerned for her safety—and with good reason," I fudged.

"And that's *all,*" he pressed.

"I didn't know the woman. I'd never seen or met her before. I said no more than a sentence or two to her."

"Why don't I believe you?"

"I have no reason to lie to you."

"Unless you're guilty of collusion."

"I already told you; I didn't know the woman."

"But you did feel a kind of kinship?"

That was a harder question to answer. "Maybe."

"You can't be more specific than that?"

"No, I can't."

"The man was viciously murdered," Baldwin reminded me.

"So was my wife."

Silence greeted that pronouncement. It was at least another ten seconds before Baldwin spoke again. "The

Russian Embassy is exerting a lot of pressure for the NYPD to wrap this case up fast."

"I wish you luck."

"You don't sound very sincere."

"I'm sure he has family somewhere who will mourn him. Just like the families of the women he killed here. Sorry, but I can't muster any real sympathy for a murderer. I have a feeling that if you were in my place, you'd feel pretty much the same."

He didn't answer, because he knew I was right.

"Was there anything about that woman you remember that might lead us to her?"

"She had on nice clothes. I figured she was a high-end hooker. If so, she probably left the city that night. I wouldn't be surprised if she left the country."

"Is that what your psychic sense tells you?"

"Just an educated guess, detective. It's what I would have done."

"But you didn't."

"I didn't need to." I didn't speak again for long seconds. "Detective Baldwin; my wife is dead and now my life is here."

"And you're sure that's all you have to tell me."

"Yes."

"Good-bye, Mr. Resnick. Have a happy, *guilt-free life.*"

I answered honestly. "I intend to."

Who writes this stuff?

The immensely popular Booktown Mystery series is what put Lorraine Bartlett's pen name Lorna Barrett on the New York Times Bestseller list, but it's her talent -- whether writing as Lorna, or L.L. Bartlett, or Lorraine Bartlett -- that keeps her there. This multi-published, Agatha-nominated author pens the exciting Jeff Resnick Mysteries as well as the acclaimed Victoria Square Mystery series, Tales of Telenia adventure-fantasy saga, and now the Lotus Bay Mysteries, and has many short stories and novellas to her name(s). Check out the descriptions and links to all her works, and sign up for her emailed newsletter here: http://www.LLBartlett.com

You can also find her on Facebook, Twitter, Pinterest, Google+, and Tumblr.

If you enjoyed Jeff Resnick: The Collected Short Stories, please consider reviewing it on your favorite online review site. Thank you!